Briar Rose and Spanking the Maid

Robert Coover is the author of some twenty books of fiction and plays, his most recent being *Noir* and *A Child Again*. He has been nominated for the National Book Award and awarded numerous prizes and fellowships, including the William Faulkner Award, the Rea Lifetime Achievement Award for the Short Story, and a Lannan Foundation Literary Fellowship. His plays have been produced in New York, Los Angeles, Paris, London, and elsewhere. At Brown University, he teaches 'Cave Writing' (a writing workshop in immersive virtual reality), and other experimental electronic writing and mixed-media workshops, and directs the International Writers Project, a freedom-to-write programme. Coover currently splits his time between the United States of America and London. *Pricksongs & Descants*, *Gerald's Party* and *Briar Rose* and *Spanking the Maid* are all published in Penguin Modern Classics.

John Banville's novels include *The Book of Evidence*, *The Untouchable* and, his latest, *The Infinities*. He won the Man Booker Prize 2005 for *The Sea*. He has written screenplays, has adapted three of Heinrich von Kleist's dramas into English, and reviews for, among others, the *New York Review of Books*, the *Guardian* and the *Irish Times*. He lives in Dublin. Awards include the *Guardian* Fiction Prize and the James Tate Black Memorial Prize. He has also received a Lannan Foundation fellowship.

ROBERT COOVER

Briar Rose and *Spanking the Maid*

with an Introduction by John Banville

PENGUIN BOOKS

PENGUIN CLASSICS

Published by the Penguin Group
Penguin Books Ltd, 80 Strand, London WC2R ORL, England
Penguin Group (USA) Inc., 375 Hudson Street, New York, New York 10014, USA
Penguin Group (Canada), 90 Eglinton Avenue East, Suite 700, Toronto, Ontario, Canada M4P 2Y3
(a division of Pearson Penguin Canada Inc.)
Penguin Ireland, 25 St Stephen's Green, Dublin 2, Ireland (a division of Penguin Books Ltd)
Penguin Group (Australia), 250 Camberwell Road, Camberwell, Victoria 3124, Australia
(a division of Pearson Australia Group Pty Ltd)
Penguin Books India Pvt Ltd, 11 Community Centre, Panchsheel Park, New Delhi – 110 017, India
Penguin Group (NZ), 67 Apollo Drive, Rosedale, Auckland 0632, New Zealand
(a division of Pearson New Zealand Ltd)
Penguin Books (South Africa) (Pty) Ltd, 24 Sturdee Avenue, Rosebank, Johannesburg 2196, South Africa

Penguin Books Ltd, Registered Offices: 80 Strand, London WC2R ORL, England

www.penguin.com

Briar Rose first published 1996
Spanking the Maid first published 1982
Published together in Penguin Classics 2011
003

Copyright © Robert Coover, 1982, 1996
Introduction © John Banville, 2011
A different version of *Briar Rose* appeared in *Conjunction 26*

Set in 10.5/13 pt Monotype Dante
Typeset by Ellipsis Books Limited, Glasgow
Printed and bound in Great Britain by Clays Ltd, Elcograf S.p.A.

Except in the United States of America, this book is sold subject
to the condition that it shall not, by way of trade or otherwise, be lent,
re-sold, hired out, or otherwise circulated without the publisher's
prior consent in any form of binding or cover other than that in
which it is published and without a similar condition including this
condition being imposed on the subsequent purchaser

978-0-141-19299-4

Introduction

Robert Coover is one of America's finest stylists, a master of elegant nuance, subtle intent and darkly subversive humour. His abiding theme, strongly discernible in these two wonderful novellas, is the gap that lies between our notions of the world and the world's stubborn and consternating reality, and, further, the way in which that reality keeps on slyly asserting itself through the intricate elaborations of myth and fairy tale. A self-conscious artist, fully aware of his vocation and ruefully accepting of its demands, he is that rarest of things, a poet in an age of prose.

Nowhere is his artistry more in evidence, and the price it exacts more amply accepted, than in *Spanking the Maid*. Fashioned in the form of an eighteenth-century handbook of sado-masochist techniques –'There are manuals for this'– it is a metaphor, exact and exhausting, of the long and painful process by which a work of art is brought into quivering existence. Any reader who cares to know just what it is like to write a novel will be well instructed here, and will come away from the experience suitably chastened, cheeks aglow from a lesson expertly administered.

As with writing, it is the relentlessness of the chastiser's enterprise that impresses, the grinding daily repetition of an action that may have started out in frenzies of desire and delight but that has hardened into the dull toils of a duty deeply resented but wholly unshirkable. The maid enters her master's bedroom anew each morning with her 'mop and bucket, broom, rags and brushes', determined that today she will perform every last little chore correctly, with rigorous exactitude, so that the man waking groggily in his bed from yet another night of confused and painful dreaming will be pleased with her, entirely pleased, and this time will not have to make her bend over and thrash her bared bottom until the welts spring up and blood is drawn.

'How did it all begin, he wonders. Was it destiny, choice, generosity? If she would only get it right for once, he reasons, bringing his stout engine of duty down with a sharp report on her brightly striped but seemingly unimpressionable hinder parts, he might at least have time for a stroll in the garden.'

But perfection, as we know, is not of this world, and probably not of any other, either. The master as much as the maid is a captive of dire circumstance. 'He is not a free man, his life is consecrated, for though he is *her* master, her failures are inescapably *his*.' As Samuel Beckett, surely one of Coover's exemplars, has it: 'Ever tried. Ever failed. No matter. Try again. Fail again. Fail better.'

Coover has much fun with his long-suffering pair, master and maid, writer and writing, artist and artefact. He has discerned the comical absurdity that is the worm in the bud of all erotic works, and tweezers it out for our amused inspection. The very idea of the artist belabouring the backside of his cowering, flawed creation is a cause for laughter, not all of it unkind, for even as we laugh we cannot but feel for the poor fellow, harassed, still half asleep and plagued by the monstrousness engendered by his unceasing struggle to *get it right*. The *fleurs de mal* of his creation are discovered each day when the maid throws back the bedcovers: 'Things that oughtn't to be there, like old razor blades, broken bottles, banana skins, bloody pessaries, crumbs and ants, leather thongs, mirrors, empty books, old toys, dark stains.' Just as daffodils and skylarks, so are such lowly things as these the stuff of art.

In *Briar Rose* the hero, as we must call him, is also bound to an endless and thankless task. The work is a set of variations, Bachian in grace and Beethovinian in vigour, on the legend of Sleeping Beauty, called here Briar Rose. This time the subject is not art – although the art of story-telling is everywhere probed and tested, challenged and mocked – but the nature of romantic love. It is about much else besides, of course, much, much else, for all true works of art are myriad-minded.

This obsessional roundelay too is funny, like *Spanking the Maid*, only funnier. Now the gap between what appears to us to be the case and what actually is becomes a chasm from which dark laughter rises. The hapless prince for all his energies is every bit as entranced and trapped as the sleeping object of his desire. Here we find him thrashing fruitlessly amidst the forest of briars that rings the castle where the enchanted damsel lies in expectation of his coming:

'Though he no longer even wishes to reach her, to wake her, he continues, compelled by vocation, to slash away at his relentless adversary, whose deceptive flowers have given the object of this quest the only name he knows. Though she remains his true love, salvation and goal, the maker of his name, jewel at the core, and all that, he cannot help but resent her just a little for getting him into this mess, which is probably fatal.'

There is not one prince but many, all of them aspects of the dreaming girl's hopes, desires, misgivings, fears. In one manifestation she cannot distinguish him from her father, in another he is the wicked fairy in disguise. In dream she senses his hands upon her, tenderly seeking out her secrets, then realizes that what she feels is not the touch of princely fingers but of the countless claws of the vermin that over the long years have come to nest in her chemise . . . And even when Charming does succeed in hacking his way through the walls of briar and penetrating the castle to where she lies, the momentous moment turns out to be a let-down. 'My prince! You have come at last! Yes, well, it was a matter of honour, he said gravely, disappointing her. I did it for the love of love.'

These two little texts, that bear themselves with such seeming lightness, have the dark resonance of folk-tales and the artful self-consciousness of modernist myth-making. The word 'classic' is much abused, but in this instance it is entirely apt. Coover is a magician, and these are his spells.

John Banville

for Pili & all her magic tricks

He is surprised to discover how easy it is. The branches part like thighs, the silky petals caress his cheeks. His drawn sword is stained, not with blood, but with dew and pollen. Yet another inflated legend. He has undertaken this great adventure, not for the supposed reward – what is another lonely bedridden princess – but in order to provoke a confrontation with the awful powers of enchantment itself. To tame mystery. To make, at last, his name. He'd have been better off trying for the runes of wisdom or the Golden Fleece. Even another bloody grail. As the briars, pillowy with a sudden extravagance of fresh blooms, their thorns decorously sheathed in the full moonlight, open up to receive him as a doting mother might, he is pricked only by chagrin. Yet he knows what it has cost others who have gone before him, he can smell their bodies caught in the thicket, can glimpse the pallor of their moon-bleached bones, rattling gently when the soft wind blows. That odor of decay is about the extent of his ordeal, and even it is assuaged by the fragrances of fresh tansy and camomile, roses, lilac and hyssop, lavender and savory, which encompass him affectionately – perhaps he has been chosen, perhaps it is his virtue which has caused the hedge to bloom – as he plunges deeper into the thicket, the castle turrets and battlements already visible to him, almost within reach, through its trembling branches.

She dreams, as she has often dreamt, of abandonment and betrayal, of lost hope, of the self gone astray from the body, the body forsaking the unlikely self. She feels like a once-proud castle whose walls have collapsed, her halls and towers invaded, not by marauding armies, but by humbler creatures, bats, birds, cats, cattle, her departed self an unkempt army marauding elsewhere in a scatter of confused intentions. Her longing for integrity is, in her spellbound innocence, all she knows of rage and lust, but this longing is itself fragmented and wayward, felt not so much as a monstrous gnawing at the core as more like the restless scurry of vermin in the rubble of her remote defenses, long since fallen and benumbed. What, if anything, can make her whole again? And what is 'whole'? Her parents, as always in her dreams, have vanished, gone off to death or the continent or perhaps to one of their houses of pleasure, and she is being stabbed again and again by the treacherous spindle, impregnated with a despair from which, for all her fury, she cannot awaken.

The pale moonlit turrets of the castle, glimpsed through the brambles, rise high into the black night above like the clenched fists of an unforgiving but stonily silent father, upon whose tender terrain below he is darkly trespassing, heralded by a soft icy clatter of tinkling bones. Unlike these others who ornament the briars, he has come opportunely when the hedge is in full bloom, or perhaps (he prefers to think) the hedge has blossomed tonight because it is he who has come, its seductive caresses welcoming him even as the cold castle overhead repels, the one a promise and a lure, showing him the way, the other the test he must undertake to achieve the object of his heroic quest. Which is? Honor. Knowledge. The exercise of his magical powers. Also love of course. If the old tales be true, a sleeping princess awaits him within. He imagines her as not unlike this soft dew-bedampened wall he is plunging through, silky and fragrant and voluptuously receptive. If she is the symbolic object of his quest, her awakening is not without its promise of passing pleasures. She is said, after all, to be the most beautiful creature in the world, both fair and good, musically gifted, delicate, virtuous and graceful and with the gentle disposition of an angel, and, for all her hundred years and more, still a child, innocent and yielding. Achingly desirable. And desiring. Of course, she is also the daughter of a mother embraced by a frog, and there has been talk about ogres in the family, dominion by sorcery, and congress with witches and wizards and other powers too dark to name. If there be any truth in these century-old rumors from benighted times, this adventure could end, not in love's sweet delirium, but in its pain, its infamous cruelty. This prospect, however, does not dissuade him. On the contrary. It incites him.

There is this to be said for the stabbing pain of the spindle prick. It anchors her, locates a self when all else in sleep unbinds and scatters it. When a passing prince asks who she is, she replies simply, having no reply other to offer, I am that hurts. This prince – if prince he be, and who can truly say as he / it drifts shapeshifting past, substantial as a fog at sea? – is but one of countless princes who have visited her in her dreams, her hundred years of dreams, unceasing, without so much as a day's respite. None remembered of course, no memory of her dreams at all, each forgotten in the very dreaming of them as though to dream them were to erase them. And yet, so often have her dreams revisited fragments and images of dreams dreamt before, a sort of recognizable architecture has grown up around them, such that, though each dream is, must be, intrinsically unique, there is an ambient familiarity about them all that consoles her as memory might, did she know it, and somewhat teaches her whereto to flee when terror engulfs her like a sudden wicked spell. One such refuge is what she sometimes supposes to be a kitchen or a servery, else a strange gallery with hearth and wooden tub, oft as not at ground level with a packed earthen floor and yet with grand views out an oriel's elevated bay. Sometimes there are walls, doors, ceilings, sometimes not. Sometimes she drifts in and out of this room alone, or it appears, in its drafty solitude, around her, but sometimes familiar faces greet her, if none she knows to name, like all else ever changing. Except for one perhaps: a loving old crone, hideously ugly and vaguely threatening, yet dearer to her in her dreams than any other, even courting princes.

Well, old crone. Ugly. Thank you very much. Has that smug sleeper paused to consider how she will look and smell after a hundred years, lying comatose and untended in an unchanged bed? A century of collected menses alone should stagger the lustiest of princes. The curse of the bad fairy, yes. She has reminded the forgetful creature of this in her dreams, has described the stagnant and verminous pallet whereon she idly snoozes and croned her indelible images of human decrepitude, has recounted for her the ancient legends of saints awaking from a hundred years of sleep, glimpsing with dismay the changes the world has suffered, and immediately crumbling into dust. Her little hearthside entertainments. Which are momentarily disturbing perhaps, causing her charge's inner organs to twitch and burble faintly, but nothing sticks in that wastrel's empty head, nothing except her perverse dream of love-struck princes. Or maybe she knows, instinctively, about the bewitching power of desire, knows that, in the realm of first kisses, and this first kiss firstmost, she *is* beautiful, must be, the fairy herself will see to that, is obliged to, must freshen her flesh and wipe her bum, costume and coiffure her, sweep the room of all morbidity and cushion her for he who will come in lustrous opulence. Alone, the fragrances at her disposal would make a pope swoon and a saint cast off, his britches afore, eternity. No, all these moral lessons with which the fairy ornaments the century's dreaming are mere fancies invented for her own consolation while awaiting that which she herself, in her ingenerate ambivalence, has ordained.

Though proud of the heroic task set him (he will, overcoming all obstacles, teach her who she is, and for his discovery she will love and honor him forever without condition) and impatient with all impediment, he nevertheless does feel impeded, and not so much by the heady blossoms' dense embrace as by his own arousal which their velvety caresses have excited. They seem to be instructing him that the prize here without may well exceed the prize within, that in effect his test lies not before him but behind, already passed, or, rather, that the test is not of his strength and valor but of his judgment: to wit, to choose an imagined future good over a real and present one is to play the fabled fool, is it not? Perhaps that tale the countryman told that put him all on fire to engage upon this fine adventure was but a subtle ruse to lure him to the briar hedge and thus into this profounder examination of his maturity and aplomb. All about him, the swaying remains of his anonymous predecessors clink and titter in the moonlight as though to mock the naive arrogance of his quest (who is he to seek to 'make his name' or to penetrate the impenetrable?) and to call him back to the brotherhood of ordinary mortals. If it feels good, do it, he seems to hear their bones whisper in wind-chimed echo of that ancient refrain, and for a moment the hostile castle turrets recede and his eyes, petal-stroked, close and something like pure delight spreads outward from his thorn-tickled loins and fills his body – but then, pricked not by briars but by his own sense of vocation, his commitment to love and adventure and honor and duty, and above all his commitment to the marvelous, his passionate desire to transcend the immediate gratifications of the flesh and to insert himself wholly into that world more world than world, bonding with it indissolubly, his name made not by single feat but by forever-aftering, he plunges forward again (those turrets: where have they gone?), wide-eyed and sword raised high.

Her ghostly princes have come to her severally with bites and squeezes, probing fingers, slaps and tickles, have pricked her with their swords and

switched her thighs with briar stems, have licked
her throat and ears, sucked her toes, spilled wine
on her or holy water, and with their curious lips
have kissed her top to bottom, inside and out, but
they have not in these false wakings relieved her
ever of her spindled pain. Often they are beautiful,
at least at first, with golden bodies and manelike
hair and powerful hands and lean rippling flanks,
yet are sad and tender in their gaze in the manner
of martyred saints; but at other times they are
doddering and ugly, toothless, malodorous and
ravaged by disease, or become so even as they
approach her pallet, a hideous transformation that
sends her screaming to the servery, if a servery is
what it is, and sometimes they become or are
more like beast than man, fanged and clawed and
merciless as monsters are said to be. Once (or more
than once: she has no memory) she has been
visited by her own father, couched speculatively
between her thighs, dressed in his crown and cloak
and handsome boots and chewing his white beard,
a puzzled expression on his kind royal face, as, with
velvety thrusts, he searches out the spindle. In her
waking life there might have been something
wrong about this, but here in sleep (she knows she

is asleep and dreaming, a century's custom having this much taught her) it hardly seems to matter and in some wise brings her comfort for he rests lightly on her and softens her cracked lips and nipples with his tears or else his moist paternal tongue, whilst he attends her mother, standing at the bedside with cloths and lotions at his service and offering her advice. Over her head, as though she were not present (and she is not), they lament the loss of their only child and worry about the altered kingdom and whether it can ever be put right again. It's that damned spindle, her mother says. Can't you do something about it? Yes, yes, I'm working on it, he gasps as his face turns red and his eyes pop open and his beard falls off.

Who am I? She wants to know. *What* am I? Why this curse of an endless stupor and its plague of kissing suitors? Do their ceaseless but ineffectual assaults really prefigure a telling one, or is my credulous anticipation (I have no memory!) merely part of the stuporous and stupefying joke? These are the sorts of childish questions the fairy must try to answer throughout the long night of the hundred-year sleep, as the princess, ever freshly distressed, heaves again and again into what she supposes to be the old castle servery or else her nursery or the musicians' gallery in the great hall, or something of each of these, yet none. Patience, child, the fairy admonishes her. I know it hurts. But stop your whinging. I will tell you who you are. Come here, down this concealed passageway, through this door that is not a door. You are such a door, accessible only to the adept, you are such a secret passageway to nowhere but itself. Now, do you see this narrow slot in the wall from which the archers defend the castle? It is called, like you, a murderess. If you peer through it, perhaps you will see the bones of your victims, rattling in the brambles down below. Like you, this slot has long since fallen into disuse, and, see here, a pretty black spider has built her web in it. You are that still creature, waiting silently for your hapless prey. You are this window, webbed in spellbinding death, this unvisited corridor, that hidden spiral staircase to the forbidden tower, the secret room at the top where pain begins. You are all things dangerous and inviolate. You are she who has renounced the natural functions, she who invades the dreams of the innocent, she who harbors wild forces and so defines and provokes the heroic, and yet you are the magical bride, of all good the bell and flower, she through whom all glory is to be won, love known, the root out of which all need germinates. You are she about whom the poets have written: The rose and thorn, the smile and tear:/The burden of all life's song is here. Do you see this old candleholder? asks the fairy, pointing to the sharp iron spike in the petaled center of the wall bracket lamp by the archers' window. She grasps a slender tallow candle the color of bedridden flesh and with a sudden violent gesture impales it on the spike, causing the sleeper to shriek and shrink away and her dormant heart to pound. With a soft cackle, the fairy lights the candle with her breath and says: You are that flame, flickering like a burning fever in the hearts of men, consuming them with desire, bewitching them with your radiant and mysterious allure. What the fairy does not say, because she does not want to terrify her (always a mess to clean up after, linens to change), is: You are Beauty. She says: When others ask, who am I, what am I, *you* are the measure and warrant of their answers.

Rest easy, my child. You are Briar Rose. Your prince will come.

He, the chosen one, as he presumes (I am he who will awaken Beauty!), presses valiantly through the thickening briar hedge, hacking without mercy at the petals that so voluptuously caress him, aware now that they were his first test and that he has perhaps lingered too long in their seductive embrace and so may have already failed in his quest, or may even have made a wrong turning and lost his way: those castle turrets, where *are* they— ?! The bones of his ill-fated predecessors clatter ominously in the assaulted branches, and the thorns, exposed by his cropping of the blossoms, snag in his flesh and shred what remains of his clothing. But he is not frightened, not very anyway, nor has he lost any of his manly resolve to see this enterprise through, for he knows this is a marvelous and emblematic journey beyond the beyond, requiring his unwavering courage and dedication, but promising a reward beyond the imagination of ordinary mortals. Still, he wishes he could remember more about who or what set him off on this adventure, and how it is he knows that his commitment and courage are so required. It is almost as though his questing – which is probably not even 'his' at all, but rather a something out there in the world beyond this brambly arena into which he has been absorbed, in the way that an idea sucks up thought – were inventing him, from scratch as it were (he is not without his lighter virtues): is this what it means 'to make one's name'? In reply, all around him, the pendulous bones whisper severally in fugal refrain: I am he who will awaken Beauty! I am he who will awaken Beauty! I am he who will awaken Beauty!

Her true prince has come at last, just as promised! He is lean and strong with flowing locks, just a little hair around his snout and dirt under his nails, but otherwise a handsome and majestic youth, worthy of her and of her magical disenchantment. She sleeps still, eyes closed, and yet she sees him as he bends toward her, brushing her breast with one paw – hand, rather – and easing her thighs apart with the other, his eyes aglow with a transcendental love. It is happening! It is really happening! she thinks as he lowers his subtle weight upon her as a fur coverlet might be laid upon a featherbed. The only thing unusual about her awakening is that it is taking place in the family chapel and she is stretched out in her silken chemise on the wooden altar, itself draped for the occasion in fine damask. Her parents are watching from the upper gallery, having just wandered in from their bedchamber, her father still pulling on his cream-colored woolen drawers, her mother dressed in a long black tunic, clasped at the throat with a ruby brooch. Below them stand the steward and the marshal and the cook and the butler and chamberlain, the entire staff of domestic servants and household knights, but they all seem to be dead. No, they are merely asleep, awaiting your own awakening, explains the old crone, midwifing her prince's kiss, who seems not to know how it is done. His mouth approaches hers and she is filled with his presence, it is as though he is melting into her body or she into his, but when in joy (the new day dawns at last!) she opens her eyes he is nowhere to be found, nor is she in the chapel nor in her sickbed either. She is in what is probably the kitchen, where the familiar old crone, her head wreathed in a flickering glitter of tiny blue lights like otherworldly fireflies, is sitting by a door that is not a door, one leading to a hidden corridor (she does not know how she knows this to be true), slitting the white throat of a trussed piglet, which is squealing madly as though for a mother who has abandoned him. Probably this has happened before, perhaps many times, she doesn't remember, can't remember. Who am I? she demands. *What* am I? The crone hangs the gurgling piglet by its trotters on a beam to let it drain and says: Calm down, child. Let me tell you a story . . .

There was once a beautiful young princess, relates the fairy, who, for reasons of mischief, her own or someone else's, got something stuck under her fingernail, a thorn perhaps, and fell asleep for a hundred years. When she woke up— What was her name? What? This princess: What was her name? Oh, I don't know, my child. Some called her Beauty, I think. That's it, Sleeping Beauty. Have I heard this story before? Stop interrupting. When she woke up— How did she wake up? Did a prince

kiss her? Ah. No. Well, not then. There were little
babies crawling all over her when she came to. One
of them, searching for her nipple, had found her
finger instead and— Babies? Yes, it seemed that
this Sleeping Beauty had been visited by any
number of princes over the years, she was a kind
of wayside chapel for royal hunting parties, as you
might say, and so there were naturally all these
babies. The one that sucked the thorn out died, of
course, and just as well because in truth she had
more of the demanding little creatures than she
and all the fairies who were helping her could
manage. She— Why were they all so little if she'd
been asleep a hundred years? Many of them must
have grown old and died meanwhile, there must
have been old dead bodies lying around. Well,
maybe it wasn't exactly a hundred years, Rose,
who's to say, maybe it was more like a long winter,
what's time to a dreamer, after all? Anyway, when
this baby sucked the thorn out, Beauty woke up
and found she suddenly had this big family to raise,
so when the princes dropped by again for the
usual, she made what arrangements were necessary
and accommodated them all as best she could,
given their modest tastes— I mean, she really

didn't have to *do* anything, did she? – and they all became good friends. And everyone lived happily ever after— ? Well, they might have if it hadn't been for the jealous wives. The princes were married— ?! Of course, what did you expect, my child? And their wives, needless to say, were fit to be tied. Finally, one day when the princes had all cantered off to war for the summer as princes do, these wives threw a big party at Beauty's place and cooked up all her children in a hundred different dishes, including a kind of hash, sauced with shredded onions, stewed in butter until golden, with wine, salt, pepper, rosemary, and a little mustard added, which they particularly enjoyed. As for Beauty, that little piece of barnyard offal, as they called her, they decided to slit her throat and boil her in a kind of toad-and-viper soup. Not very nice, but they were so jealous of her they didn't even want her to taste good. Besides, their stomachs were full, the soup would be used to feed the poor. And that's the end of the story? Well, almost. Beauty had been given a lot of pretty presents by her princes, as you can imagine, for they all loved her very much, and they included some lovely gowns in the latest fashion, stitched with gold and silver thread and trimmed with precious jewels, which the wives now fought over, screeching and biting and clawing in the royal manner. They raised such a din that even their princes, far away at war— But it's *terrible!* She would have been better off not waking up at *all!* Well. Yes. I suppose that's true, my dear.

He enters her bedchamber, brushing aside the thick dusty webs of a lost century. She lies more upon the bed than in it, propped up in overflowing silks and soft wools and elegant brocades, and delicately aglow in the dusky room as though her unawakened spirit were hovering on her surface like some sort of sorcelous cosmetic. Is she wearing anything? No. Or, rather, yes, a taffeta gown perhaps, deep blue to set off her unbound golden hair, which flows in lustrous rivulets over the feather pillows and bedding and over her body, too, as though to illuminate its contours. Her matching slippers are not of leather but also of a heavy blue silk and her stockings, gartered at the knees, are of the purest white. Of course, dark as it is, he might not be able to see all this, though, as he imagines it, dawn is breaking and, as he pushes aside the ancient drapes (he has already, hands now at her knees, pushed them aside, they turned to dust at his touch), the rising sun casts its roseate beams upon her, and especially upon her fair brow, her faintly flushed cheeks, her coral lips, parted slightly to receive his kiss. He pauses to catch his breath, lowers his sword. He has been hacking his way feverishly through the intransigent briar hedge, driven on by his dreams of the prize that awaits him and by his firm sense of vocation, but, far from turning to dust at his touch, the hedge has been resisting his every movement, thickening even as he prunes it, snatching at him with its thorns, closing in behind and above him as he advances, if advancing is what he has truly been doing. He should have reached the castle walls long ago. Did he, distracted by the heady blossoms, make a wrong turning, and is he now circling the walls instead of moving toward them? It is impossible to tell, he is utterly enclosed in the briars, could not see the castle turrets even were they still overhead, which, he feels certain (clouds have obscured the moon, all is darkness), they are not. Perhaps, he thinks with a shudder, I have not been chosen after all. Perhaps . . . Perhaps I am not the one.

Well, everyone *might* have lived happily ever after, replies the old crone, gutting a plucked cock, if it hadn't been for his jealous wife. He was married— ?! Of course, my love, what did you think? And she was, as you can imagine, a very unhappy lady, even if perhaps she was not the ogress everyone said she was, her husband especially. But that's terrible! That's not the worst of it, I'm afraid. I don't know if I want to hear the rest. She is in the kitchen, which at first was more like her parents' bedchamber or else the bath house, listening to the ancient scold in there tell a story about a princess who fell into an enchanted sleep as a child and woke up a mother. The princess is called Sleeping Beauty, though that might not have been her real name. Has she heard this story before? She can't remember, but it sounds all too familiar, and she is almost certain something bad is about to happen. But she goes on listening because she cannot do otherwise. So she waited until her husband was off hunting or at one of his other houses of pleasure, the old crone continues, ripping out the cock's inner organs, and then she went over to Sleeping Beauty's house and cooked up her children and ordered the clerk of the kitchen to build a big bonfire and burn Beauty alive, calling her a cruel homewrecking bitch and a lump of you-know-what. The kitchen hag, cackling softly, squeezes a handful of chicken guts, making them break wind. There is something vaguely reassuring about this, not unlike a happy ending. The prince's wife, the crone continues, her hands braceleted in pink intestines, had in mind serving up a very special roast to her husband when he got home, believing, you see, that the way to a man's heart is, heh heh, through the stomach. She sniffs at the cock's tail. The story seems to be over. And that's all? she demands in helpless rage. Not quite, smiles the crone. She shakes her old head and a swarm of blue lights rises and falls around her ears. Sleeping Beauty was wearing a beautiful jewel-studded gown her friend the prince had given her and his wife wanted it, so she ordered Beauty, before being thrown on the fire, to strip down, which she did, slowly, one article at a time, shrieking wildly with each little thing she removed, as though denuding herself was driving her crazy. Meanwhile, as she'd hoped, the prince was just returning from whatever he'd been up to and, on hearing Beauty scream, came running, but before he knew it he found himself in the middle of a huge briar patch. Oh no! Oh yes! He had to cut his way through with his sword, redoubling his effort with each cry of his poor beloved, but the briars seemed to spring up around him even as he chopped them down, and the more she screamed and the more he slashed away, the thicker they got. Yes, yes, I can see him! No, you can't, he was completely swallowed up by the briars. A pity, but it was too late. No! Hurry! Here I am! It's *not* too late!

He is caught in the briars. The gnarled branches entwine him like a vindictive lover, the thorns lacerate his flesh. Everywhere, like a swampy miasma: the stench of death. He longs now for the solace of the blossoms, their caresses, their fragrance. Ever life's student, he reminds himself that at least he has learned something about the realm of the marvelous, but it does not comfort him. Nothing does, not even fantasies of the beautiful sleeper who lies within, though he does think of her, less now in erotic longing than in sympathetic curiosity. He is young but has adventured the world over, while she, though nearly a century his senior, knows only a tiny corner of a world that no longer even exists, and that but innocently. What kind of a thing is this that jumps about so funnily? she is said to have asked just before being pricked by the fatal spindle and falling into her deep swoon. And now, what if no one ever reaches her, what if she goes on dreaming in there forever, what sort of a life would that be, so strangely timeless and insubstantial? Yet, is it really any different from the life he himself has until now led, driven by his dream of vocation and heroic endeavor and bewitched by desire? Ah, the beautiful: what a deadly illusion! Yet, still he is drawn to it. Still, though all progress through the hedge has been brought to a painful halt and the thorns tear at him with every stroke, he labors on, slashing determinedly at the hedge with his sword, beating back the grasping branches, and musing the while upon this beautiful maiden, fast asleep, called Briar Rose. Does she ever dream of her disenchantment? Does she ever dream of him?

★

Certainly, she dreamt of her sweetlipped prince all the time, says the fairy, in reply to Rose's question. But that was not who finally kissed her awake. No? No, in the end she was taken rather rudely by a band of drunken peasants who had broken into the castle, intent on loot. I don't believe this. Of course you believe it, says the fairy. You have no choice. They thought she was dead and commenced to strip her of her finery and naturally one thing led to another and they all had a turn on her, both before she was kissed and after. As the poet put it: Lucky people, so 'tis said, / Are blessed by Fortune whilst in bed. But that's *terrible!* The dreaming child has come to her, fleeing a nightmare about being awakened by an old administrator of her father's kingdom, a stuffy and decrepit ancient with fetid breath, and the fairy has told her an antidotal story about Sleeping Beauty (Have I heard this story before? Rose wanted to know), one of several in the fairy's repertoire, this one with a happy ending. Of course, when the ruffians woke up Beauty they also woke up everything else in the castle, down to the flames in the hearth and the flies on the wall, and including the household knights, who captured the thieves and made them eat their own offending privates before hanging them in the courtyard as an edifying entertainment for the domestic servants, failing to realize that, in effect, they were at the same time severally widowing the poor princess, soon heavy with child. And that was how, fatherless, Dawn and Day were born. Rose is clearly not consoled by this story. She's had enough, she cries. She wants to wake up. Why me? she demands. Why am I the one? It's not fair!

Caught in the briars, but still slashing away valiantly, driven more by fear now than by vocation, he seeks to stay his panic with visions of the sleeping princess awaiting him within, as much in love with her deep repose as with any prospect of her awakening. He has imagined her in all states of dress and undress and in all shapes and complexions, spread out inertly like soft bedding on which to fall and take his ease or springing ferally to life to consume him with her wild pent-up passion, but now he thinks of her principally as a kind friend who might heal his lacerations and calm his anguished heart. It's all right, nothing to fear, dear love, lie back down, it's only a nightmare. Ah, would that it were so! he gasps aloud, his voice sucked up into the dense black night, his desperate heroism's only witness. He pauses to pluck the stinging thorns snagged in his flesh and is immediately pricked by dozens more as the briar hedge, woven tight as a bird's nest, presses up around him. He's not even sure his feet are still on the ground so painfully is he clasped, though he still wears his boots at least, if little else of his princely raiment remains. At times he doubts there is really anyone in the castle, or that there is even a castle, those ghostly turrets glimpsed before notwithstanding. Or if there is a castle and a waiting one within, perhaps it is only the bad fairy who set this task for him and for all these dead suitors, defined their quest with her legendary spite and spindle, this clawing briar hedge the emblem of her savage temper, her gnarled and bitter soul. And even if there is a princess, is she truly the beautiful object of pure love she is alleged to be, or is she, the wicked fairy's wicked creature, more captor than captive, more briar than blossom, such that waking her might have proven a worse fate than the one that is seemingly his, if worse than this can be imagined?

She dreams of her handsome prince, cutting his way through the torturous briars and heroically scaling the high castle walls to reach her bedside and free her from this harsh enchantment. Or perhaps she thinks of him doing so: what, in her suspended condition, is the difference? In either case, there is no residue. Always when she thinks of him, or dreams of him, it is as if for the first time, though she doubts that it can be, there being little else to fill the vast hollow spaces of her pillowed skull but such thoughts, such dreams, and though she remembers very little, she does remember remembering. Moreover, each awakening seems to be enacted against a field of possible awakenings, and how can she know what is possible, even if it is not possible, without, in some manner, remembering it? What she does remember, or believes she does, is being abandoned by her parents on her fifteenth birthday, so little did they care for her and all the omens cast upon her, leaving her once again to her own lonely explorations of the drafty old castle, explorations which have since provided the principal settings for all her dreams, or thoughts, but which on that day led her up a winding staircase to the secret room at the top of the old tower, there to meet (she remembers this) her cruel destiny. It's not fair. Why was she the one? It was nothing bad she had done, she was famous for her goodness, if anything it was for what she'd not done, having aroused the wrath of malefic powers, envious of her goodness and her beauty, or so her ancient friend in the servery tells her now when she complains, as she has, as she's told now, so often done. You are one of the lucky ones, the old crone says, wagging a gnarled finger at her. Your sisters were locked away in iron towers, lamed and stuck in kitchens, sent to live with savage beasts. They had their hands and feet cut off, were exiled, raped, imprisoned, reviled, monstrously deformed, turned to stone, and killed. Even worse: many of them had their dreams come true. My sisters? Yes, well, long ago. Dead now of course.

Her dreamtime moral lessons: out one ear and out the other, as the saying goes. In spite of all the fairy's promises and reprimands, when the little ninny's not bewailing her fate, she's doubting it, or if not doubting, dreading it, afraid of what she longs for. It's frustrating, she simply cannot, will not learn, and it sometimes makes the fairy, haunting too long this empty head, lose her temper, even though she knows that could she, would she, her own magical ends would surely be thwarted. That the child sometimes fears what she most desires, the fairy can appreciate, princely heroes being the generally unreliable and often beastly lot that they are, but that she doubts that her prince will ever come suggests she underestimates her own legendary beauty and its power to provoke desire in men. That such desire is a kind of bewitching (no wonder they blame it on the fairies!), the fairy knows and uses to her frequent advantage, though just how it actually works is something of a mystery to her, one of the main differences between humankind and fairies being that, for fairies, to desire something is to possess it. The nearest she can come to it is desiring desire itself so as to know the seeming pleasure got from its withheld satisfaction. She is not all-powerful, of course, and so sometimes suffers as well a certain ephemeral longing for the more absolute powers denied her, but, as a caster of spells and a manipulator of plots, the fairy understands that her talents by their very nature assume other powers and prior plots which provide the necessary arena for her transactions; it might even be said that she is empowered by the very powers she lacks, so she cannot really desire them. If, for example, in order to experience desire and its gratification firsthand, she were to try to take Rose's place in the bed and receive her prince (unlike Rose, she *can* learn, *would*), she knows she might lose power over her spell and either reveal herself prematurely or get trapped in her new role with no way to escape it. In a sense, omnipotence is a form of impotence. No, a stool in the servants' quarters of this mooncalf's head where she can sit quietly, filing her teeth, is the closest the fairy can come to witnessing desire's strange mechanisms, or, passing fancies apart, would wish to.

She is awakened by a band of ruffians, all having a go on her lifeless body, sometimes more than one at a time. At first she believes, she doesn't know why, that they are drunken peasants who have invaded the castle to loot it, but she soon discovers, recovering somewhat her foggy wits, that they are her father's household knights. They seem more dead than alive, ghostly pale, drooling, their eyes rolled up, showing only the whites. They have roped her to the bedposts, there is no escape, so she leaves her struggling there and goes looking for her ancient friend in the servery, if that's what it is, perhaps it is the great hall, or even the chapel. Oh mother, she groans, why am I the one? Because you won't listen! cries the ill-tempered old scold, flinging the carcass of a plucked goose at her. I'm sorry, child, she says then, picking up the feather-less bird and sending it flying out the oriel bay window as though to right a wrong, I didn't mean that, I know you can't help it, but, believe me, you should stop complaining, you are one of the lucky ones. And, poking around in her leathery old ear with a blackened claw as though to dig the story out of there (what comes out are more of those little blue lights like a swarm of sparkling nits), she tells her about a poor princess married to a wild bear who smelled so bad she had to stuff pebbles up her nose. He pawed her mercilessly and took her violently from behind and bit her when he mated and scratched her with his great horny claws. But the worst thing was his she-bear. He was married— ?! Of course, you silly booby, what did you think? The old crone's ferocious tale seems to come alive and she is lying with the stinking bear while his enraged wife snarls and bares her sharp teeth and snaps cruelly at her exposed parts. Why are the crone's stories always about, you know, the natural processes? she asks, though she does not know why she knows this to be so, 'always' itself a word whose meaning eludes her. Because, grunts the bear, who seems to be trying to push another painful spindle into her from behind, she's merely an enchantress, my love, it's all the old hag knows.

Not true; though, true, it's what she's best at, feelings and perceptions the very gestures of her intimate art, the foolish passions of the world-beguiled what best she can get her iron teeth into. But the prison of the flesh is not her only theater, the wheel of sensuous agony and delight not her one and only turn. She is also, in her waggish way, a devotee of the higher learning, an interpreter and illuminator, concerned with truth and goodness and, above all, beauty, the mind her stories' true domain, body merely their comic relief. Though reputed to carry a sack of black cats on her back and to delight in slitting open the tums of indolent girls and stuffing them up with scurf and rubble, she prefers in fact to provision their desolate heads, ravaged by ignorance and sentiment, and what she carries on her back, alas, is the weight of eternity, heavy as a cartload of cowshit. A mere hundred years? It's nothing, you ninny, she replies to the sniveling dreamer, really you are one of the lucky ones. And she tells her the story of the princess chained to a rock thousands of years ago (it seems like only yesterday!) and guarded by a fire-breathing sea monster, who could never understand why this wailing creature, so ruinously chafed by wind and tide, should be thrust upon him like some kind of unanswerable riddle. Well, nothing to do but eat the bony little thing, he supposed, compelled less by appetite than by the mythical proprieties, and he was just tucking dutifully in when a prince turned up intent on rescue, so the dragon asked him in effect the question you have asked. He, too, had no sequential memory, knew only that he was born, so they said, of chaos, she of love, and thus they were cosmological cousins of a sort, and should bear no grudge against one another, so how had they arrived at this moment of mortal encounter, which seemed more theoretical in nature than practical? The prince, well schooled, was interested in this question, touching as it did on the sources of the heroic quest, about which he too sometimes had his misgivings, but the dragon's breath was so hot and noxious all he could do was gasp that it not only always comes down to a family story in the end, but it's always the same one. The monster gaped his jaws in awe of this wisdom and the prince fired a fatal arrow down his throat and into his doubting heart. And they lived happily ever after? How could they, the dragon was dead. No, I mean the princess and the – Oh, who can say? The prince had other tasks and maidens to attend to, making a name for himself as he was, for all I know, my dear, that one's chained there still.

★

Inextricably ensnared in the briars, yet never ceasing to resist (he will remain a hero to the end), he attempts to conjure up an image of the legendary princess who waits inside (but not for him), hoping to assuage his terrible pain and disappointment and stay his rising panic, but it is not her incomparable radiance and beauty that appear to his imagination but more cadaverous traits: her deathly pallor, sunken flesh, crumbling gown, her empty eye sockets. And the ghastly silence that reigns over her. Oh no! Too late! He wets her shrunken bosom with his tears, strokes her cold cheeks, gazes with horror upon her dreadful inertness. He turns her over: her backside is eaten away, crawling with worms and – no, he does not turn her over! He hacks desperately at the brambles and, as the hedge closes round him like the grasping flesh-raking claws of an old crone, imagines instead her dreams, sweet and hopeful and, above all, loving: loving him who is to come, slashing through the briars and scaling the castle walls to reach her bedside with his spell-unbinding kiss. She does not yet dream of that dream-dissolving kiss, however, but rather of his excitement when he discovers her there in all her resplendent innocence, her unconscious body at the mercy of his hungry gaze and impassioned explorations before he quickens it with his kiss, his excitement and her own unwilled passivity before it exciting her in turn, making her eager to awaken and not to awaken at the same time, so delightful is this moment, though of course, he may not be there yet, it is no simple matter to scale the sheer walls of the castle, many have fallen, and once inside he might get lost in the maze of halls and stairs and corridors, not knowing for certain where to find her, and there might be other sleepers along the way who attract his kisses, not to mention his excited explorations, delaying him until it is too late, and even before he can get to the walls there is the infamous briar hedge, noisy with the windblown clatter of bones, the bones of those for whom commitment to love, adventure, honor, and duty and a firm sense of vocation were not enough, their names unmade, forever-aftered into the ignominious anonymity of the nameless dead. No! he cries. Don't just lie there! Get up! Come help!

Her charge has just emerged from a nightmarish awakening in which she was kissed by a toad and turned into one herself and as usual has come running, so to speak, to the fairy, who is calming her with a tale about a beautiful young princess who got pricked one day by a spindle and fell asleep for a hundred years. Have I heard this story before? Hush, child. When she woke up, she found two little babies suckling at her breasts, and one of them – Babies— ?! Yes, it seems that her prince, or some prince anyway, had been visiting her person regularly over the years, and these— But didn't the prince kiss her? Didn't he break the spell and wake her up? Well, he may have, I don't know, that's not part of this— But that's *terrible!* Already she had these babies and she didn't even know if she'd been kissed or not— ?! I *hate* this story! All right, wait a minute, let's say he did. He came into the room, greeted the fairies, played with little Dawn and Day, and kissed the princess. That's it? Now what's wrong? It doesn't sound right. It's not like a real story. What do you know about it, you little ninny? snaps the fairy, picking up one of the children and smacking its bottom to, making her point, make it cry: Whose story is this anyway? Rose takes the baby away from her and cuddles it. You really are very wicked, she says, rocking the baby gently in her arms to stop its screaming, and the fairy cackles at that. You're right, she says, when she woke up there weren't any children, that's a different story. Rose stares confusedly into her arms, now cradling empty air. I don't mind, she says timorously, you can leave the babies in if you want. No, no, there were no babies, forget that. Beauty woke up and found not one prince beside her bed, but three: a wizened old graybeard, a leprous hunchback with a beatific smile, and the handsome young hero of her dreams. Which one of you kissed me awake? Beauty asked, looking hopefully at the pretty one. We all did, replied the oldtimer in his creaky voice, and now you must choose between us. Take the holy one, he said, pointing to the scurvy hunchback in his haircloth, and your life will be lost to the self deceiving confusions of human compassion; take the other and you must live all your life with lies, deceit, and unrestrained wickedness. That may be true, old man, said the beautiful one with a snarling curl of his lip, but at least I'm not so hard of heart as you. And I live in the real world of the senses, not some chilly remote tower of the mind. Look at this! He stripped off his princely finery and, with a flourish, watching himself in a round gilt-framed mirror on the wall, struck a pose worthy of the great classic sculptors, with that funny thing between his legs hopping like a frog. Ah, but remember, said the leper, opening his robes and, as though in parody, peeling off a wafer of flesh from his diseased chest, physical beauty is only this deep and lasts but a brief season, while spiritual beauty lasts forever. So tell me, my love, says the fairy, scratching her cavernous armpits, which did Sleeping Beauty choose? Oh, I don't know, whines Rose, and I don't care. You're just making my head ache. Tell me about the babies again.

Her prince has come at last, his clothing shredded from his ordeal in the briars, his stained sword drawn. He slips the blade under her thin gown, grown fragile over the long century of waiting, and with a (her eyes are closed, but she sees all this, knows all this, feels the cold blade slide up her abdomen and between her breasts, watches it lift the gown from her body like a rising tent) quick upward stroke slices it apart. She lies there in all her radiant innocence, exposed to the mercy of his excited gaze, excited by his excitement and by her own feeling of helplessness (she can do nothing about what happens next), and then he kisses her and she awakes. My prince! she sighs. Why have you waited so long? But he has turned away. The room is full of household knights and servants and they are all applauding, her mother and father among them, clapping along with the rest. He sheathes his sword, accepts their cheers and laughter with a graceful bow, blows kisses at the ladies. They gather around him and, chattering gaily, lead him away, fondling his tatters. He does not even look back. Abandoned, she wraps her naked shame in her own hug and drifts tearfully into the nursery or the kitchen, looking for consolation or perhaps some words of wisdom (maybe there are some babies around), but finding instead a door that is not a door. She opens it to the hidden corridor on the other side, which leads, she knows (it's all so familiar, perhaps she wandered here as a child), to a spiral staircase up to a secret tower. Passing the slotted archers' window, she pauses to wonder: is he out there somewhere in the briars? More important: is he really *he*? She climbs the staircase, which winds round and round, up, up, into the shadowy tower above, so high she cannot see from up here where she began below. At the top, behind a creaky old door, she finds a spinning room and an old humpbacked woman in widow's garb, sitting there amid a tangle of unspooled flaxen threads like a spider in her web. Ah, there you are, my pretty, the old crone says, cackling softly. Back for more of the same? Who *am* I? *What* am I? she demands angrily from the doorway, fearing to enter, but fearing even more to back away, uncertain that the stairs she has climbed are still there behind her. It's not fair! Why am I the one?

Hopelessly enmeshed in the flesh-rending embrace of the briars, he consoles himself with thoughts of what might have been: the legendary princess, his brave overcoming of all obstacles to arrive at her bedside and disenchant her with a magical kiss (he has a talent for it, women have often told him so), her soft expectancy and subsequent adoration of him, his fame and hers and the happiness that must naturally flow therefrom. Around him, the tinkling bones of those nameless brothers he'll soon join speak to him of the vanity of all heroic pursuits and of the dreadful void that the illusions of immortality, so-called, cannot conceal. Well, of course, all life affirmations are grounded in willing self-delusion, masks, artifice, a blind eye cast toward the abyss, this is the very nature of heroism, he knows this, he doesn't need the bones to tell him. Yet still, mad though it may be, he longs to write his name upon the heedless sky. Still (he slashes, a branch falls; it grows back, doubly forked; rearmed, he slashes again), he must strive. If he were now to reach her bedside and, with his bloody lips, free her from her living death, he would tell her that he did it for love – not for love of her alone, but for love of love, that the world not be emptied of it for want of valor. Would that disappoint her? No, she would understand, she was Beauty, after all, chosen as he was chosen, or as he'd thought he'd been (damn!), and so would know that his kiss, their love, their fated happiness, existed on a plane beyond their everyday regal lives, that theirs has been an emblematic ordeal and a redemption shared with the world. Yes, all right, but it wasn't much of a kiss. What— ?! I mean, it was hardly more than a little peck, I didn't even feel it. It was like you really didn't mean it. Oh, he sighs, slashing away bitterly, I guess my mind was elsewhere.

When she awakens, he is fondling her excitedly, his excitement exciting her (she pleases him!), his touches, too (and he her!), her body tingling with his feverish explorations. It's better even than she imagined it. His delicate hands are everywhere, lightly scrambling up and down her body, it's almost as though he has more than two of them, and he is lashing her with a soft woolly whip, now her thighs, now her face, now her breasts. She smells sweet fennel, balm, lavender, and mint, mixed with dust and less pleasant odors, and she recognizes the smell from her childhood: the rushes strewn with the aromatic herbs on the great hall floor, where she often played beneath the trestle tables while her elders ate. Whom she now hears above her, laughing uproariously. She opens her eyes and sees the monkey perched on her chest between her breasts, smirking at her under the miniature crown tied under his chin. He pinches one pink nipple in his bony little fingers, lifts it and shakes it like a bell, his lips splitting in a maniacal grin, and she feels the ripples all the way to the depths of her belly, where a dull insistent pain resides. Her mother and father and all their friends and all the knights and servants of the castle are gathered around, gazing down with greasy-faced delight upon this spectacle, hooting and laughing and slapping their thighs. They have been eating and drinking, many are eating and drinking still, chewing, spitting, guzzling, and the refuse from their feast is all about her. The monkey rises on all fours, turns his back, lifts his tail to display to her his waxen crimson bottom, and commences to lick and paw between her legs as though picking fleas or searching for something to eat. She feels a burning itch there which she wants desperately to scrub, but she can't move a finger, it's as though all but her intimate parts have been turned to stone. She is terrified and humiliated, but she is also strangely thrilled, not only by the monkey's frolicsome two-handed rummaging, but also by the outrage being committed upon her here, the flaunting of proprieties, the breaking of royal taboos. It's like something is being released, and it feels almost explosive. If only the monkey would stop tickling her and (though she doesn't know

what 'it' might be) get on with it! That seems to
spring a new burst of laughter from her audience,
but she is certain she did not speak aloud, cannot.
She cannot even cry out as the monkey, losing his
temper and snatching and digging at her furiously,
slapping, clawing, biting, finally shoving a whole
arm inside her, brings back, redoubled, the spindled pain. It's almost as though he wants to break
her open, get at what's down deep inside! This is
terrible! Why are they all laughing?! She's hurting
so— ! Just then, thankfully, a familiar old crone
wanders through, shoos the monkey away (the
revelers are gone, vanished, her mother and father
among them, as though they never were), melts
her petrified limbs, restores her voice to her: Was
that it? Has it happened? Has the spell been broken?
she gasps, clutching her assaulted parts with both
hands. The crone does not reply (they are in the
servery now, or maybe the nursery), but instead,
cackling softly, says: Calm down, my precious. Let
me tell you a story.

Once upon a time, the fairy relates, there was a
rather wild and headstrong little girl who, ignoring

the warnings of her elders, climbed up to the top of a secret tower where an old woman was spinning, got pricked by a spindle, and fell asleep for a hundred years. What was her name? I don't know, don't interrupt. It was me, wasn't it? No, Rose, this was someone else. Her name was Beauty, I think. Have I heard this story before? Hush, now! When her hundred years were up, she was awakened by a handsome young prince who loved her very much and visited her whenever he could get away from his wife, which was usually about once every fortnight. He was married— ?! Of course he was. Didn't I just tell you? I must have forgotten. But didn't it make her very unhappy – I mean, after waiting all that time— ? Yes, it did, but she understood that, being from the last century, she was probably a bit old-fashioned, while he was a modern prince with different ideas, and anyway she had no choice. When the prince's wife, who was an ogress, found out about the affair, she waited until the prince had gone off hunting one day, and then she went over to Beauty's house and ordered the clerk of the kitchen to strip off Beauty's finery, which the wife naturally wanted for herself and without any nasty stains on it, thank you, then to slit her throat and roast her on a spit over the fire. Meanwhile, she prepared a rich garlic soup with spicy fish dumplings, fresh leeks broiled in butter and black pepper, cabbage stuffed with sausage and seasoned with vinegar, mustard, saffron, ginger, and herbs from the garden, fresh baked bread, and for dessert a blancmange flavored with anise. When her husband came back from hunting and saw what she had done, he was very upset of course, Beauty was a special favorite of his, having helped him make his name and all, but he was also very hungry and his wife, who was a wise ogress, had brought along a big jug of delicious young wine from the south to go with the feast she'd prepared, so in the end he settled down and enjoyed his meal, even if he did find the meat a bit tough, being more than a century old as it was. As the ogress had never been able to have any children of her own, she and the prince adopted Beauty's little orphans and took them home with them and they all lived happily ever after. Rose is not amused by this story. It was nothing like that, she complains. What do you know about it, you silly creature? demands the fairy. It is not easy, keeping this going for a hundred years, and she does not appreciate her charge's dismissive attitude. It just doesn't sound right, Rose says. Real stories aren't like that. Real princes aren't.

Her prince has come. The real one. It is dark and she does not know where she is but she knows he has come and that it is he. She is filled with rejoicing, but also with trepidation. So much is at stake! She has known all along that her prince would come, but she has also known there would be no uncoming, forever after as much a threat as promised delight. What if he is not as she's imagined him to be? She was safe inside this impenetrable castle, protected even from the demands of her own body, and now this alien being who paces at her bedside has broached those walls and will soon break through to her very core, if he has not already done so. All her childhood fears return: of the dark, of strange noises, of monsters and ghosts, of murderers, of being left alone, of her parents dying, of getting sick and dying herself, of the world dying. He clears his throat. Has he kissed her yet? She doesn't remember, but she musters her courage and opens her eyes to see who or what is there, terrified now that she will find a great hairy beast prowling beside her bed. But, no, it is he, a handsome young prince with manly brow and beard and flowing locks, tall and lean and strong. My prince, she whispers. You have come at last! Yes, well, he says with a grimace, wandering distractedly through the dimly lit room, draped in swags of gray dusty webs, which he swipes at irritably with his gauntleted hand. At a wooden chest, he picks up a bonehandled copper pitcher enameled with the family crest, thumps it, peers at its green bottom, sets it down again. He pokes through some wardrobe drawers, raising clouds of dust, finds some rings and necklaces and silver pennies, which he sorts through idly. Perhaps he takes some of these things, but not as a thief might: in effect, he *possesses* them. With one metallic finger he strokes a plump lute resting on a table: the dry strings snap and ping, their ancient tension released, but not hers. My prince? He turns his restless gaze upon her for a moment and then it seems to pierce right through her, as though focusing on something within or beyond her, chilling her to the marrow before it drifts away again, coming to rest on a chessboard with cracked and yellowed ivory pieces. He moves one of the figures, freeing it from its bonds of web, then, with a shrug, tips it over. It is a delicate, casual, yet studied gesture, and it terrifies her. In front of a round dust-grimed mirror on the wall, he stares at himself, stroking his beard. He is immaculately groomed and dressed, more elegant even than she had dreamt he would be. You are very beautiful, she murmurs timidly, but I thought you'd, I don't know, show more outward signs of your terrible ordeal. Ordeal— ? You know, the briars. He turns away from the mirror, peers at her warily with narrowed eyes. What briars? Didn't you have to cut your way through a briar hedge outside? Maybe, he says stonily, I'm at the wrong castle.

He has, in his imagination (all that's left him), slashed his way through the briars, scaled the castle wall, and reached her bedside. He had expected to be aroused by the mere sight of her, this legendary beauty both doelike and feral, and indeed, stripped naked by the briars, his flesh stinging still from the pricking of the thorns which he seems to be wound in now like a martyr's shroud, he is aroused, but not by the grave creature who lies there before him, pale and motionless, wearing her ghostly beauty like an ancient ineradicable sorrow. His sense of vocation propels him forward and, pushed on by love and honor to complete this fabled adventure, he leans forward to kiss those soft coral lips, slightly parted, which have waited for him all these hundred years, that he might unbind her from her spell and so fulfil his own emblematic destiny. But he hesitates. What holds him back? Not this hollow rattle of old bones all about. Something more like compassion perhaps. What is happily ever after, after all, but a fall into the ordinary, into human weakness, gathering despair, a fall into death? His fate to be sure, whether he makes his name or not (what does it matter?), but it need not be hers. He imagines the delirium of their union, the celebrations and consequent flowering of the moribund kingdom, the offspring that would follow, the joys thereof, the pains, the Kingship, the Queenship, her obligations, his, the days following upon days, the exhaustion of the 'inexhaustible fountain of their passion,' the disappointments and frustrations and betrayals, the tedium, the doubts (was it really she after all? was it really he?), the disfigurements of time, the draining away of meaning and memory, the ensuing silences, the death of dreams; and, enrobed in pain, willfully nameless, yet in his own way striving still, he slips back into the briars' embrace.

The fairy sits spinning in the tower, entangled in her storied strands, joining thread to thread, winding them into seductive skeins, awaiting the dreamer's visit, her accusations, her demands. It has not been easy, trying to fill her limboed head through all this time, by some calendars as much as a century or more, so from time to time over the years (call them that), in order to rehearse her craft, re-spell the wound, she has returned here to the source. The scene, as they say, of the crime. Of course, given the child's inability to put any two thoughts together in succession or to hold either of them between her ears longer than it takes to think them, the fairy might just as well tell the same story over and over again, and indeed she has repeated most of them, one time or another, it has been a long night. But, for her own

sake more than her auditor's, fearing to lose the
thread and sink away herself into a sleep as deep
as that she inhabits, thus gravely endangering them
both, she has sought, even while holding fast to
her main plot, to tell each variant as though it had
never been told before, surprising even herself at
times with her novelties. She has imagined, and
for Rose described, a rich assortment of beauties
and princes, obstacles, awakenings, and what-
happened-nexts, weaving in a diverse collection
of monsters, dragons, ogres, jests, rapes, riddles,
murders, magic, maimings, dead bodies, and
babies, just to watch the insatiable sleeper wince
and gasp and twitch with fear and longing, wicked
fairy that she is. She has rarely gone afield in her
tales, wandering instead the tranced castle, using
it some times as a theatrical contrivance, others as
a kind of house of the dead, touring intimately its
most secret recesses. Castle-bound as the dreamer
is, the illusion of boundaries, above all that of the
body, has been one of the fairy's frequent themes,
along with the contest between light and dark,
the passions of jealousy and desire, cannibalism,
seduction and adultery, and the vicissitudes of
day-to-day life in the eternal city of the tale, the

paradoxes thereof. That between gesture and language, for example. This she illustrated one day, when asked, But why does he have to *kiss* her, by describing in exhaustive detail every nuance of the sleeper's expression as witnessed by the hovering prince, down to the subtle chiaroscuro of light as it grazed her brow at different angles and the movement of the fine hairs in her nostrils, a cartographical epic that might have gone on without lips meeting lips for the rest of the century, had not her capricious audience, screaming for release, retreated in spite to a passing nightmare about a prince who awoke her by sinking his teeth suddenly into her throat.

Though he no longer even wishes to reach her, to wake her, he continues, compelled by vocation, to slash away at his relentless adversary, whose deceptive flowers have given the object of this quest the only name he knows. Though she remains his true love, salvation and goal, the maker of his name, jewel at the core, and all that, he cannot help but resent her just a little for getting him into this mess, which is probably fatal. She is beautiful, true, perhaps the most beautiful creature in the world, or so they say, and, in his agony, he has consoled himself with thoughts about her, principally of an amorous nature, it being that sort of adventure, but he has also thought often about his life before he undertook this quest, its simple sensible joys, the freedom of it, the power he wielded, the fame and honor he enjoyed, even if all much less than her disenchantment might have provided, had he been the one chosen for it. He has imagined, having first imagined the eventual success of this enterprise, explaining to her, or trying to explain, his continuing attraction to that former life in order to suggest a distinction between his breaking of her spell and the happily-ever-after part, the latter to be negotiated separately, and, so doing, has grasped something of the true meaning of her name, for clearly, from her perspective, this hundred years' wait has not prepared her to tolerate such a distinction. In short, at the least hint of his choosing other than the either of her either/or, she has seemed prepared (in his imagination) to scratch his eyes out. Which in turn has offered him an insight into a possible way out of here: could it be that, in struggling against the briars, he might in fact be struggling only against something in himself, and that therefore, if he could come to understand and accept the real terms of this quest, the briars might simply fade away? Or is that what all these other clattering heroes thought?

She has told her (the little dimwit has forgotten this, perhaps she will tell it again) about the prince who, trapped in the briars, was given three wishes and wasted them by first wishing himself in Beauty's bedroom, which he found empty, then wishing to know where she was, and, on learning she was in the very hedge he'd been trapped in, wishing himself back in the briars again, though the wishes weren't completely wasted because at least now, on a clear day when their shouts carried, he had company in his suffering. The fairy recognizes that many of her stories, even when by her lights comic, have to do with suffering, often intolerable and unassuaged suffering, probably because she truly is a wicked fairy, but also because she is at heart (or would be if she had one) a practical old thing who wants to prepare her moony charge for more than a quick kiss and a wedding party, which means she is also a good fairy, such distinctions being somewhat blurred in the world she comes from. Thus, her tales have touched on infanticide and child abuse, abandonment, mutilation, mass murder and cruel executions, and, in spite of the subjects, not all endings have been happy. She has told her the story of the musicians at Beauty's wedding feast who distracted the bride with their flutes and tambourines and kettledrums, while their dancing girls were off seducing the groom, thereby sending him to his nuptial bed with a dreadful social disease. She has told her (also forgotten) of a monstrously evil Sleeping Beauty and of the horrors unleashed upon the prince and all the kingdom when he awakened her, as well as of the hero under a beastly spell who ate Beauty immediately upon finding her so as to avoid returning to his dreary life as a workaday prince, adding a few diverting notes about his digestive processes just to stretch the tale out. But stories aren't like that, the ill-tempered child will inevitably insist, and the fairy only cackles sourly at that and tells another. She will be up here soon. Now she's found the way, she cannot help but keep coming back. But it always takes her a while to find it. Rose imagines this ancient spinning room in the tower to be an impossible distance away, through hidden corridors and up rickety stairwells, not realizing that it is, so to speak, just behind her left ear . . .

When he finally, with a last desperate stroke, slashed through and emerged from the dark night of the briars, he found that day had broken and the world had changed. He'd evidently lost his way inside the hedge and got turned around, for there was his horse, still tethered where he'd left him. But the forest he'd tethered him in was gone. Everything was gone. As far as he could see: a vast barren landscape under the noonday sun. A fairy came, the horse explained, and took everything away. What—? The horse could talk—? Of course it could talk, says the old crone irritably, peering up at her from her spinning wheel. What's wrong with that? I don't know, it just doesn't seem right. She wonders if her own prince could have a talking

horse, and since, in her stuporous condition, thinking and speaking are the same thing, the crone
replies: A talking horse? Don't be ridiculous! Why
do you always suppose every story is about you?
Now come on in here and stop interrupting. She
remains in the drafty doorway, afraid to enter
(something bad has happened here) but afraid to
back away, uncertain if the spiral staircase she has
climbed is still there behind her. She does not like
this story, but knows that its teller knows this
without her having to say so. Little blue sparks fly
as the crone, turning the wheel slowly, lets the flax
slide through her old gnarled fingers. The prince,
she continues, wanted to know what the fairy
looked like, what color was she, how many teats
did she have, was she good or bad, did she come
from outside or inside? Inside what? asked the
horse. The hedge, stupid, said the prince with an
impatient gesture. But then he saw that the hedge
was gone, too, they were all alone in the blazing
emptiness. He thought about this for a moment,
and then he said: Maybe everything is really still
here. Maybe it only appears to our bewitched
senses to be gone. That may seem reasonable to
you, snorted his horse, but it doesn't make my

kind of sense. No, really, insisted the prince, it's one of the fairies' favorite tricks. So maybe now, knowing this, I can finally get through to the hidden castle and break the spell. Is this possible? Can he do it? Her interest in the story has picked up, and she takes a tentative halfstep into the room, bringing a curling smile to the dry lips of the old crone. So the prince raised his sword and, bracing himself for the worst, went charging about under the hot sun like one possessed, hoping to bump up against something solid, but in the end all he got out of it was sunblindness and a terrible thirst. The horse snickered at all this human folly and said they should move on and try to find something to eat, but the prince, who was on a heroic quest which he felt determined to see through to the end, even if seeing was no longer what he did best, stubbornly refused, so the horse trotted off without him. The prince went on frantically hunting for the invisible castle for the rest of his life, which was not long, there being nothing to eat in that desert but sand. He died— ? Oh yes, raisined up like a dogturd out there in the sun, my pet, a worshipful sight. They would have made him a saint, but they didn't know what to call him since he had failed in his quest and so had never made his— No, she insists from the doorway, backing away. You can't do that. That's not how stories are.

The more the possibility of reaching her bedside recedes, the closer he seems to come to her. He does not know if, consumed by fear and desire, he is generating this illusion himself, or if it is fairy magic. But he is scaling the castle walls before he has escaped the briars, exploring the castle before he has scaled the walls. It feels as if an impossible problem is being solved, all by itself. The castle itself is a strange and haunted place, unlike any he has ever seen before, yet also oddly comforting, more like home than home. Searching for her through its webby mazes, he feels like he is opening doors to his own past, though it is more like a past that might have been than a real one. Before he has found her, he is already at her bedside. He is so stunned by her beauty, he can't move, even though his lips are already approaching hers. He thinks: Won't it all be spoiled if I wake her up? But he has already awakened her: they are in the great hall, or else in front of the oriel window, gazing out on the manicured gardens, bordered by a small trimmed hedge of sweetbriar. She is just as he has imagined her: beautiful, gentle, innocent, devoted, submissive. He is suffused with love and desire, but he also feels like he would like to take a nap. Today, she says, I saw a strange thing. I saw a plucked goose flying. It flopped into my room where I was sleeping or else lying awake and said to me: You will never awaken because the story you were in no longer exists. Oh yes? He is thinking about the quest that brought him here. Has he made his name then? If so, what is it? Or has he perhaps come to the wrong castle? When she says, perhaps not for the first time, that, even when sitting in the same room with him, she feels like she's all alone, he realizes his mind has been elsewhere. I'm sorry, my love, he says. What is your heart's desire? To live happily ever after, she replies without emotion. Of course, he replies, it's yours for the asking. And also I wonder if you'd mind watching the babies for a while? Babies— ?!

★

She is in the kitchen, or else the nursery, playing with the babies. They seem to have been conjured up by one of the old crone's tales, but she's glad they're there, strange as they are, more like her parents than any children, the boy with his little tuft of beard, the girl gazing upon her in haughty disapproval even as she changes her breechcloth. The crone, stirring a thick steamy brew in a cauldron big as a bathtub, hung over the fire on an iron chain (they *are* in the kitchen then, or else in the bedchamber and that *is* a bathtub), is telling her a story about a princess guarded by a fire-breathing dragon known for his ferocity and his insatiable appetite for tender young maidens, breath-roasted while spitted on a claw. The crone provides several of the dragon's favorite recipes for basting and dipping sauces, which Rose does not find amusing. Usually – if one with a memory such as hers can really have any idea about what might be usual – she is alone in the castle with the old crone, but sometimes it is full of other people, servants, knights, even princes, and the children come and go at random (they are gone now), an arrangement which also somewhat perplexes her, though only when she imagines she is awake, not often. Today she was fooled by a prince who approached her bedside and began probing her as though examining her systematically for the source of her spindled pain. He was tall and handsome, but badly wounded, his clothing shredded and clinging to him by bloody tatters. My prince! You have come at last! Yes, well, it was a matter of honor, he said gravely, disappointing her. I did it for the love of love. But what kind of a thing is that that jumps about so funnily? she added sleepily, although it was not what she had meant to say at all, it just seemed to pop to mind. For providing relief from sorrow and contact with the numinous, he replied tersely, even as his fingers burrowed deeper. Though it is all an illusion of course. Yes, I know, she sighed and opened her eyes. No prince. Of course. Just a family of nesting churchmice, scurrying beneath her gown. She closed her eyes again and, without transition, found herself here in the kitchen, where now the old crone is down on her haunches, adding a few sticks of firewood to the embers and fanning them into flames with her thick layers of smelly black skirts. In her story, the hero has just flown in with the head of a lady with snaky hair that turns everyone into statues.

He aims the frightful thing at the dragon, but the dragon ducks and looks away and the head stuns the princess instead. Now she's useless to everyone. She may have heard this story before, the part about a princess turned to stone is familiar, but she can't be sure. What was the princess's name? she asks. Don't interrupt! snaps the old crone, shaking the slotted spoon at her, sparks flying from her clashing teeth, her wild unkempt hair twisting about her head like a nest of vipers. She ladles something out of the cauldron that looks like another baby. The important question, you little ninny (her own knees and elbows have gone numb, perhaps she has been lying too long in the same position), is whose head was he using?

Searching in himself for the magical knowledge that might make the murderous briars sheathe their thorns and fade away, he has seemed to hear the sleeping princess say (perhaps this is just before awakening her, or perhaps it is years later): There is a door that is not a door. That is where it all begins. He knows that nothing at this castle is simply what it is, everything here has a double life, so he supposes she is trying to tell him something else, the way out of this thorny maze, for example, or the way in to her own affections. She is in front of a mirror (the doubled redoubled), letting down her golden hair. Her beauty numbs him. Now that I am awake, she says, the truth is more hidden than before. Her mirrored eyes meet his: When will this spell be broken? she asks. When will my true prince come? So, as he feared: he is not the one. Or perhaps he is the one, or could be, this her plea that he become the prince she has been dreaming of. He does indeed feel himself becoming that imagined prince, and he wonders if perhaps she is a sorceress. His doubts darken her countenance, either with sorrow or with anger. Or with desire. She holds the mirror up to his face and he sees something hairy and toothy, halfway between a wolf and a bear, and he feels overwhelmed by lust and stupidity, a not unpleasant sensation, the best he's had probably since he set forth upon this adventure. It doesn't last, forget happily ever after, she is dressing him in pretty new clothes with all the needles left inside and leading him by the paw into the great hall for the castle ball. As he enters the hall, engulfed in pain, he realizes he has arrived at the perilous edge of the world and that from this entering there will be no departing. Help! he howls. Wake up! Get me out of here!

She imagines him (a conjuring of sorts) somehow scaling the unscalable walls and, his flesh stinging still from the barbed briars, searching through the webbed labyrinth of the ancient castle for the bedchamber of the legendary sleeping princess, but finding instead a door that is not a door, leading down a secret corridor to a spiral staircase. He climbs it, sword drawn, and, in a room at the top of the tower, finds a beautiful maiden with flaxen hair spinning alone by candlelight. Ah, there you are! she exclaims breathlessly. You have come at last! That's strange, I was told you would be sleeping, he says. I couldn't wait, she replies with a seductive smile. Now come on in here and close the door, you're letting in a draft. He hesitates, framed by an abysmal darkness, his sword still drawn, then looks away, keeping her only in the corner of his eye, no doubt hoping to catch her changing back to her real shape when she thinks she is not being watched. Ah, nothing worse, from the fairy's point of view, than a cogitative prince. Brave and handsome, yes, and perhaps a few of the social graces, a smooth dancer, comfortable with the clichés: Charming, as they're so often called. But not too much introspection, thank you, not too much heavy pondering, else the game's up for distressed maidens like her present seeming self, who weeps now as though her heart has been broken. You don't love me! she sobs. You are not the one! Yes, I am! he cries, sheathing his sword and rushing to her side. I'm sorry, my love! He falls to one knee and clasps her to his wounded bosom. That's better. But it's so hard to know what's real and not in such a place, he pleads. I know, I know, she groans, hugging him tight, pressing the thorns in deeper. She has one hand between his legs, peeling away the bloody tatters that remain. I'm such a silly goose, she sighs, smiling tenderly at him, her iron teeth, she knows, glinting like nuggets of gold in the guttering candlelight, a voluptuous sight not even she, in his boots, could resist. Then, with a rueful sigh (such is the fairy's lonely burden!), she unravels the knots, loosing thread from thread, and, allowing her hump to rise once more, her hide to hornify, her multitude of breasts to fall, commences to spin again. Desire: what is it exactly?

She is seated beside the king at the high table in the great hall. He looks like her father, yet is not her father. There is something heavy weighing on her head which makes her want to lie down under the table and go to sleep. She touches it: a crown. A great span of time seems to have passed since her awakening, which she cannot at the moment remember. Or, more likely, she is still asleep and dreaming, this merely another of the old crone's wicked entertainments. The room is full of banqueters and servants but they are not moving or speaking. Perhaps they have been turned to stone. Two naked children, who may be hers, are playing in the dirty rushes under the trestle tables, their rosy bottoms bobbing like apples in a tub of dirty water, the only things moving in the hall. She would like to give them both a good spanking, or else go play with them (she could be the dragon), but she is too tired to move. Happily ever after, the king says. It's never quite like you imagine it. She nods. A mistake.

The weight of her crown carries her head all the way into her plate of food. She has, literally, to lift her head with both hands and put it upright on her shoulders again. Time disfigures everything, he sighs and belches, scratching his hairy belly. But at least we have our memories. We do? An ancient humpbacked creature shuffles in from the kitchen and gives her a cloth with which to wipe the gravy from her face. One of the old crone's petticoats, by the smell of it. Of course we do. Don't you remember the musical parade at our wedding feast, this crowned and bearded stranger asks, the flutes and trumpets, the kettledrums, the tambourines? No . . . The dancing girls? She flies into a sudden rage and wheels round to dig her nails into his face, her crown toppling. She claws deep red grooves through his cheeks. He does not resist. You are not the one! she screams. His beard, catching the rivulets of blood, seems to whiten as though a century were passing. Sometimes, he says, gazing at her tenderly as if indeed he might know her or have known her once upon a time, I feel the reason I never escaped the briars was that, in the end, I loved them, or at least I needed them. Let's say, he adds with a curling smile, licking at the blood at the corners of his lips, they grew on me . . .

Although still trapped in the hedge, he has somehow clawed his way through, scaled the castle walls, awakened the sleeping princess, broken the spell, and saved the moribund kingdom. Even the flies, they say, got up off the wall and flew again. But it all happened so long ago, his memory of it is as though a borrowed one, and he feels substantially unrewarded for all his pain and suffering. Which she, for one (the entire kingdom is another), has never truly appreciated, taking it all for granted as part of the devotion due her. Or else doubting it altogether, as she doubts him: Are you really the one? she will ask from time to time, gazing darkly at him with fear and suspicion. Perhaps not, he thinks, licking his unhealed wounds. Perhaps I have come to the wrong castle. When he first arrived here, or imagined arriving here, it was like returning home again, so familiar was it. He knew, for example, even before escaping the briars, just where the sleeping princess lay. But it may be that his knowing was itself part of the spell, for the castle has grown in strangeness ever since. Or perhaps he has grown more complex, his quest less clear and pure, the castle recognizable only to an unmazed mind. He can no longer even find at will her sleeping chamber, though he is often in it, transported there as though by sorcery when simplified by desire and wine, or by his terror of the briared night. What happens there is a periodic reminder to him of the brevity of all amorous pursuits and the symmetries of love and death, and seems intended to recall for him, or perhaps for her, that night he is said to have first awakened her: the stale morbidity of the bed in which she lay, canopied in dark dusky webs, its linens eaten by the vermin scurrying within, she spread upon it like a sentient bolster, so sweetly vulnerable, hands crossed primly on her pubescent breast, knees together, the rouge of her cheeks and the coral of her parted lips like painterly touches of the embalmer's art, her gown a silky gauze turned by time to dust that vanished in a puff when he blew upon it, or so she has told him, explaining the powdering of her body and what he must do now to please her. These nightly rituals pass like dreams, or rather like a single dream redreamt, so indistinguishable are they from one another, which also seems a portion of her pleasure. Yes, yes, that's how it was! Her obsessive recreations of love's awakening delirium are perhaps what most oppress him, not because, as he blows the dust away, they cast a shadow of what might have been upon their workaday royal lives, but because they suggest to him what might yet, if he could but escape this castle, be. He hears rumors of enchanted princesses out on the perilous fringe, asleep for a hundred years or more, and longs to ride out once again on new adventure, to tame mystery and make his name in the old way, but she does not understand such restlessness, she was born to these stacked stones, so haunted by her dreams, it's all the life she knows or wants to know, heroic endeavor a kind of wickedness to her, all quests but one unholy. When he makes the mistake of announcing to all present at high table in the great hall his noble intention to sally forth to rescue another sleeping maiden, she explodes with sudden fury, clawing at his face as though to scratch his eyes out, and then, just as suddenly, falls asleep with her face in the soup, provoking a general alarm. The chamberlain hauls her out of the soup by her golden hair and the sauce cook throws water on her, her lady-in-waiting unlaces her corsets and rubs her temples with eau de cologne, the chaplain slaps her hands and the kitchen boy her face, but nothing wakes her. He can feel their hostility mounting, the hairs bristling on his snout and back. His wounded face burns with pain and chagrin. I'll never get out of here, he laments. The others circle round, their faces going slack, eyes narrowing to dark bloody slits. All right, all right, he barks irritably, lifting her up and carrying her out of the great hall toward her bedchamber. I'll do it!

She awakens to repeated awakenings as though trapped in some strange mechanism, and she longs now to bring it to a standstill, to put an end once and for all to all disquiet, even if it means to sleep again and sleep a dreamless sleep. And so she goes in search of an old crone who has befriended her, one she believes may have magical powers, or at least some useful pharmaceutical ones, and while looking for her she comes upon a door that is not a door. She knows, though she does not know how she knows, that beyond it there is a long dark corridor leading to a spiral staircase, at the top of which, in the highest tower of the castle, is a spinning room. Where something bad happened. Or will happen. But something perhaps that she desires. She steps through into the secret corridor and there discovers her true prince in all his manly radiance embracing a scullery maid. Oh, sorry, he says. But she was asleep and I was only trying to— She wants to scratch his eyes out, but he has already disappeared. She seems to hear galloping hooves, though it may be only the clattering of her unhappy heart. Perhaps he has abandoned her forever, returning to his ogress wife or riding off to new adventures. It is easy for him. She has no horse, could not steer it if she did, would not know where to take it if she could, this castle all she knows or dares to know. Such a ninny, as the old crone says. But his exuberance frightens her, his worldly heroics do. He is young enough to be her great-great-great grandson, yet he seems a hundred years older. Sometimes I think it was better when we was all asleep, mum, the maid says wistfully, hands cupped under her belly, swollen with child.

I had such pretty dreams then. Yes, I know. She will have the girl's throat slit tomorrow and serve her up to him when he returns, his unborn between her jaws like a baked apple, if tomorrow ever comes, but for now, feeling like an abandoned child, those who might protect her from the fairy's curse gone off to their houses of duty or pleasure, she continues her lonely explorations, down the shadowy corridor and up the swaying spiral staircase, her eyes closed, hands crossed demurely on her breast, her silken gown disintegrating in the chill draft, lips parted slightly to receive what fate awaits her.

The bad fairy, who is also the good fairy, returning to the source as she so often does, finds her unhappy charge sprawled on the floor of the spinning room, clothed in little more than tangled flaxen strands and furiously stabbing herself over and over with the spindle. Ah, such a desire to sleep again, the fairy muses, reckoning the poor creature's tormented thoughts. She could well change herself into a handsome prince and give her a consolatory kiss and a cuddle, but, in the state she is in, it might only provoke her into throwing her disembodied self down the stairwell, augmenting her confusion and despair. Will this spell never be broken? Rose wants to know. The warring sides of the fairy's own nature clamor for attention: isn't it time to dip into your necromantic bag of tricks for a little relief, you old bawd, a bit of allegorical hocus-pocus perhaps, that old scam? The good fairy's boon to this child, newborn, was to arrange for her to expire before suffering the misery of the ever-after part of the human span, the wicked fairy in her, for the sake of her own entertainment, transforming that well-meant gift to death in life and life in death without surcease. And, in truth, she *has* been entertained, is entertained still. How else pass these tedious centuries? Once upon a time, she says with a curling smile, her wicked side as usual taking over, there was a handsome prince and a beautiful princess who lived happily ever after. But that's *terrible!* cries Rose. No, no, wait, that's just the beginning. But I *hate* this story! Happily ever after, admonishes the fairy, wagging a gnarled finger the color of pig iron. It may not be worth a parched fig, my daughter, but it hides the warts, so don't be too quick to throw it out! You really are evil, Rose groans, continuing to stab herself without mercy. Yes, well, what did you expect, you little ninny? But put that spindle down. Haven't I told you a thousand times – ? She ignores her, hammering away at the center of her pain like some strange mechanism gone amok, so the fairy turns the spindle into a slimy green frog that squirts out of her hand and, croaking frantically like one escaping a thorny entrapment, hops away, leaving Rose weeping pathetically, now utterly forlorn. All right then, my love. Listen up. Once upon a time . . .

From his dais chair at the high table he has announced to everyone in the great hall that he has heard of another enchanted princess, some leagues distant, who has slept for a hundred years, and that he now intends to ride out to find her and, if possible, to break the ancient spell. As a royal prince, dedicated to virtuous exploits of this nature, it is the least he can do, for the sake of the stricken kingdom as much as for the maiden. So, pushed on by love and honor, he has kissed his wife good-bye (or would have, had she let him) and sallied forth to confront evil, tame mystery, make his name. At the castle gates, he encounters an old webfooted hunchback who gives him a boon and a prophetic warning. Her boon is a magic ointment that will drive off wicked sorceresses and also restore hair, heal unnatural wounds, and revive manly vigor. The warning is: Take along the old weird's head, when you approach the enchanted bed. And she seems to take off her own and offer it to him. He laughs, confident of his own princely powers, and the crone, cackling along with him, disappears as though suddenly turned to dust. He journeys for many years, following the conflicting advice of countrymen met on the way, until he arrives at an enchanted forest near the edge of the world and is directed to a dark gloomy castle, said to be haunted by spirits and ogres and to contain in its depths a sleeping princess who has lain there as though dead for a hundred years. Yes, I know, that is why I am here, he says. It is my vocation. Over the years, brambles have grown up around the castle, leaving only the pale moonlit turrets and battlements visible. It will not be easy, but this, too, he has anticipated, for the pursuit of a noble quest, he knows, is ever arduous and fraught with peril. He tethers his steed, draws his sword, and steps boldly into the dense overgrowth without looking back. Fortunately, he has arrived when the thicket is in full bloom. He has left the crone's ointment back in his saddlebag, but he won't need it, even were it what the old fraud claimed it to be: the branches part gently, the fragrant petals caress his cheeks. He is surprised how easy it is. How familiar. He feels, oddly, like he's coming home again. It is not the castle, no, nor the princess inside (perhaps he will reach her and disenchant her with a kiss, perhaps he will not; it matters less than he'd supposed), but this flowering briar patch, hung with old bones, wherein he strives. I am he who awakens Beauty, the bones seem to whisper as the blossoms enfold him.

She lies alone in her dusky bedchamber atop the morbid bed. Perhaps she has never left it, her body anchored forever here by the pain of the spindle prick, while her disembodied self, from time to time, goes aimlessly astray, drifting through the castle of her childhood, in search of nothing whatsoever, except perhaps distraction from her lonely fears (of the dark, of abandonment, of not knowing who she is, of the death of the world), which gnaw at her ceaselessly like the scurrying rodents beneath her silken chemise. If she is still asleep, it does not feel like sleep, more like its opposite, an interminable wakefulness from which she cannot ease herself, yet one that leaves no residue save echoes of an old crone's tales, and the feeling that her life is not, has not been a life at all. Sometimes, in her wanderings, she finds a castle populous with sleepers, frozen in their tracks, snoring pimply-faced guards clutching wineglasses in which the dregs have dried, round-bellied scullery maids sweeping, their stilled labor swagged in thick dusty webs, the cook with a fistful of the kitchen boy's hair, his cuffing stopped in sudden sleep. But if she opens her eyes again, the castle will be dark and empty, hollow with a chill wind blowing, or else suddenly filled with a bustling confusion of servants, knights, children, animals, husbands or lovers, all making demands upon her, demands she cannot possibly fulfill, or even understand, and all she longs for, as she tells the old crone in the tower, is to sleep again. The crone may cackle or tell a story or scold her for her self-absorption, but sooner or later she will open her eyes and find herself here in her moldy bed once more, waiting for she knows not what in the name of waiting for her prince to come. Of whom, no lack, though none true so far of course, unless in some strange wise they all are, her sequential disenchantments then the very essence of her being, the fairy's spell binding her not to a suspenseful waiting for what might yet be, but to the eternal reenactment of what, other than, she can never be. She closes her eyes to such a cruel fate, but, as always, it is as if she has opened them again, and now to yet another prince arriving, bloodied but exultant, at her bedside. She welcomes him, cannot do other, ready as always for come what may. He leans toward her, blows her dessicated gown away. Yes, yes, that's right, my prince! And now, tenderly if you can, toothily if need be, take this spindled pain away . . .

SPANKING THE MAID

She enters, deliberately, gravely, without affectation, circumspect in her motions (as she's been
taught), not stamping too loud, nor dragging her
legs after her, but advancing sedately, discreetly,
glancing briefly at the empty rumpled bed, the
cast-off nightclothes. She hesitates. No. Again. She
enters. Deliberately and gravely, without affectation, not stamping too loud, nor dragging her
legs after her, not marching as if leading a dance,
nor keeping time with her head and hands, nor
staring or turning her head either one way or
the other, but advancing sedately and discreetly
through the door, across the polished floor, past
the empty rumpled bed and cast-off nightclothes
(not glancing, that's better), to the tall curtains
along the far wall. As she's been taught. Now, with

a humble yet authoritative gesture, she draws the curtains open: Ah! the morning sunlight comes flooding in over the gleaming tiles as though (she thinks) flung from a bucket. She opens wide the glass doors behind the curtains (there is such a song of birds all about!) and gazes for a moment into the garden, quite prepared to let the sweet breath of morning blow in and excite her to the most generous and efficient accomplishments, but her mind is still locked on that image, at first pleasing, now troubling, of the light as it spilled into the room: as from a bucket . . . She sighs. She enters. With a bucket. She sets the bucket down, deliberately, gravely, and walks (circumspectly) across the room, over the polished tiles, past the empty rumpled bed (she doesn't glance at it), to draw open the tall curtains at the far wall. Buckets of light come flooding in (she is not thinking about this now) and the room, as she opens wide the glass doors, is sweetened by the fresh morning air blowing in from the garden. The sun is fully risen and the pink clouds of dawn are all gone out of the sky (the time lost: this is what she is thinking about), but the dew is still on every plant in the garden, and everything looks clean and bright. As will his room when she is done with it.

He awakes from a dream (something about utility, or futility, and a teacher he once had who, when he whipped his students, called it 'civil service'), still wrapped in darkness and hugged close to the sweet breast of the night, but with the new day already hard upon him, just beyond the curtains (he knows, even without looking), waiting for him out there like a brother: to love him or to kill him. He pushes the bedcovers back and sits up groggily to meet its challenge (or promise), pushes his feet into slippers, rubs his face, stretches, wonders what new blunders the maid (where is she?) will commit today. Well. I should at least give her a chance, he admonishes himself with a gaping yawn.

Oh, she knows her business well: to scrub and wax the floors, polish the furniture, make the master's bed soft and easy, lay up his nightclothes, wash, starch, and mend the bedlinens as necessary, air the blankets and clean the bathroom, making certain of ample supplies of fresh towels and washcloths, soap, toilet paper, razor blades and toothpaste – in short, to see that nothing be wanting which he desires or requires to be done, being always diligent in endeavoring to please him, silent when he is angry except to beg his pardon, and ever faithful, honest, submissive, and of good disposition. The trivial round, the common task, she knows as she sets about her morning's duties, will furnish all she needs to ask, room to deny herself, a road (speaking loosely) to bring her daily nearer God. But on that road, on the floor of the bathroom, she finds a damp towel and some pajama bottoms, all puddled together like a cast-off mop-head. Mop-head? She turns and gazes in dismay at the empty bucket by the outer door. Why, she wants to know, tears springing to the corners of her eyes, can't it be easier than this? And so she enters, sets her bucket down with a firm deliberation, leans her mop gravely against the wall. Also a broom, brushes, some old rags, counting things off on her fingers as she deposits them. The curtains have been drawn open and the room is already (as though impatiently) awash with morning sunlight. She crosses the room, past the (no glances) empty rumpled bed, and opens wide the glass doors leading out into the garden, letting in the sweet breath of morning, which she hardly notices. She has resolved this morning – as every morning – to be cheerful and good-natured, such that if any accident should happen to test that resolution, she should not suffer it to put her out of temper with everything besides, but such resolutions are more easily sworn than obeyed. Things are already in such a state! Yet: virtue is made for difficulties, she reminds herself, and grows stronger and brighter for such trials. '*Oh, teach me, my God and King, in all things thee to see, and what I do in any thing, to do it as for thee!*' she sings out to the garden and to the room, feeling her heart lift like a sponge in a bucket. '*A servant with this clause makes drudgery divine: who sweeps a room, as for thy laws, makes that and th'action fine!*' And yes, she can still recover the lost time. She has everything now, the mop and bucket, broom, rags and brushes, her apron pockets are full of polishes, dustcloths and cleaning powders, the cupboards are well stocked with fresh linens, all she really needs now is to keep – but ah! is there, she wonders anxiously, spinning abruptly on her heels as she hears the master relieving himself noisily in the bathroom, any *water* in the bucket—?!

He awakes, squints at his watch in the darkness, grunts (she's late, but just as well, time for a shower), and with only a moment's hesitation, tosses the blankets back, tearing himself free: I'm so old, he thinks, and still every morning is a bloody new birth. Somehow it should be easier than this. He sits up painfully (that divine government!), rubs his face, pushes his feet into slippers, stands, stretches, then strides to the windows at the far wall and throws open the tall curtains, letting the sun in. The room seems almost to explode with the blast of light: he resists, then surrenders to, finally welcomes its amicable violence. He opens wide the glass doors that lead out into the garden and stands there in the sunshine, sucking in deeply the fresh morning air and trying to recall the dream he's just had. Something about a teacher who had once lectured him on humility. Severely. Only now, in the dream, he was himself the teacher and the student was a woman he knew, or thought he knew, and in his lecture 'humility' kept getting mixed up somehow with 'humor,' such that, in effect, he was trying, in all severity, to teach her how to laugh. He's standing there in the sunlight in his slippers and pajama bottoms, remembering the curious strained expression on the woman's face as she tried – desperately, it seemed – to laugh, and wondering why this provoked (in the dream) such a fury in him, when the maid comes in. She gazes impassively a moment (yet humbly, circumspectly) at the gaping fly of his pajamas, then turns away, sets her bucket down against the wall. Her apron strings are loose, there's a hole in one of her black stockings, and she's forgotten her mop again. I'd be a happier man, he acknowledges to himself with a wry sigh, if I could somehow fail to notice these things. 'I'll start in the bathroom,' she says discreetly. 'Sir,' he reminds her. 'Sir,' she says.

And she enters. Deliberately and gravely, as though once and for all, without affectation, somewhat encumbered by the vital paraphernalia of her office, yet radiant with that clear-browed self-assurance achieved only by long and generous devotion to duty. She plants her bucket and brushes beside the door, leans the mop and broom against the wall, then crosses the room to fling open (humbly, authoritatively) the curtains and the garden doors: the fragrant air and sunlight come flooding in, a flood she now feels able to appreciate. The sun is already high in the sky, but the garden is still bejeweled with morning dew and (she remembers to notice) there is such a song of birds all about! What inspiration! She enjoys this part of her work: flushing out the stale darkness of the dead night with such grand (yet circumspect) gestures – it's almost an act of magic! Of course, she takes pleasure in *all* her appointed tasks (she reminds herself), whether it be scrubbing floors or polishing furniture or even scouring out the tub or toilet, for she knows that only in giving herself (as he has told her) can she find herself: true service (he doesn't have to tell her!) is perfect freedom. And so, excited by the song of the birds, the sweet breath of morning, and her own natural eagerness to please, she turns with a glad heart to her favorite task of all: the making of the bed. Indeed, all the rest of her work is embraced by it, for the opening up and airing of the bed is the first of her tasks, the making of it her last. Today, however, when she tosses the covers back, she finds, coiled like a dark snake near the foot, a bloodstained leather belt. She starts back. The sheets, too, are flecked with blood. Shadows seem to creep across the room and the birds fall silent. Perhaps, she thinks, her heart sinking, I'd better go out and come in again . . .

At least, he cautions himself while taking a shower, give her a chance. Her forgetfulness, her clumsiness, her endless comings and goings and stupid mistakes are a trial of course, and he feels sometimes like he's been living with them forever, but she means well and, with patience, instruction, discipline, she can still learn. Indeed, to the extent that she fails, it could be said, *he* has failed. He knows he must be firm, yet understanding, severe if need be, but caring and protective. He vows to treat her today with the civility and kindness due to an inferior, and not to lose his temper, even should she resist. Our passions (he reminds him-

self) are our infirmities. A sort of fever of the
mind, which ever leaves us weaker than it found
us. But when he turns off the taps and reaches for
the towel, he finds it damp. Again! He can feel
the rage rising in him, turning to ash with its
uncontrollable heat his gentler intentions. Has she
forgotten to change them yet again, he wonders
furiously, standing there in a puddle with the cold
wet towels clutched in his fists – or has she not
even come yet?

She enters once and for all encumbered with her
paraphernalia which she deposits by the wall near
the door, thinking: it should be easier than this.
Indeed, why bother at all when it always seems to
turn out the same? Yet she cannot do otherwise.
She is driven by a sense of duty and a profound
appetite for hope never quite stifled by even the
harshest punishments: this time, today, perhaps it
will be perfect . . . So, deliberately and gravely, not
staring or turning her head either one way or the
other, she crosses the room to the far wall and with
a determined flourish draws open the tall curtains,
flooding the room with buckets of sunlight, but

her mind is clouded with an old obscurity: When, she wants to know as she opens wide the glass doors to let the sweet breath of morning in (there are birds, too, such a song, she doesn't hear it), did all this really begin? When she entered? Before that? Long ago? Not yet? Or just now as, bracing herself as though for some awful trial, she turns upon the bed and flings the covers back, her morning's tasks begun. 'Oh!' she cries. 'I beg your pardon, sir!' He stares groggily down at the erection poking up out of the fly of his pajama pants, like (she thinks) some kind of luxuriant but dangerous dew-bejeweled blossom: a monster in the garden. 'I was having a dream,' he announces sleepily, yet gravely. 'Something about tumidity. But it kept getting mixed up somehow with –' But she is no longer listening. Watching his knobby plant waggle puckishly in the morning breeze, then dip slowly, wilting toward the shadows like a closing morning glory, a solution of sorts has occurred to her to that riddle of genesis that has been troubling her mind: to wit, that a condition *has* no beginning. Only *change* can begin or end.

★

She enters, dressed crisply in her black uniform with its starched white apron and lace cap, leans her mop against the wall like a standard, and strides across the gleaming tile floor to fling open the garden doors as though (he thinks) calling forth the morning. What's left of it. Watching her from behind the bathroom door, he is moved by her transparent earnestness, her uncomplicated enthusiasm, her easy self-assurance. What more, really, does he want of her? Never mind that she's forgotten her broom again, or that her shoe's unbuckled and her cap on crooked, or that in her exuberance she nearly broke the glass doors (and sooner or later will), what is wonderful is the quickening of her spirits as she enters, the light that seems to dawn on her face as she opens the room, the way she makes a maid's oppressive routine seem like a sudden invention of love. See now how she tosses back the blankets and strips off the sheets as though, in childish excitement, unwrapping a gift! How in fluffing up the pillows she seems almost to bring them to life! She calls it: 'doing the will of God from the heart!' *'Teach me, my God and King, in all things thee to see,'* she sings, *'and what I do in any thing, to do it as for thee!'*

Ah well, he envies her: would that he had it so easy! All life is a service, he knows that. To live in the full sense of the word is not to exist or subsist merely, but to make oneself over, to *give* oneself: to some high purpose, to others, to some social end, to life itself beyond the shell of ego. But he, lacking superiors, must devote himself to abstractions, never knowing when he has succeeded, when he has failed, or even if he has the abstractions right, whereas she, needing no others, has him. He would like to explain this to her, to ease the pain of her routine, of her chastisement – what he calls his disciplinary interventions – but he knows that it is he, not she, who is forever in need of such explanations. Her mop fairly flies over the tiles (today she has remembered the mop), making them gleam like mirrors, her face radiant with their reflected light. He checks himself in the bathroom mirror, flicks lint off one shoulder, smoothes the ends of his moustache. If only she could somehow understand how difficult it is for me, he thinks as he steps out to receive her greeting: 'Good morning, sir.' 'Good morning,' he replies crisply, glancing around the room. He means to give her some encouragement, to reward her zeal with praise or gratitude or at least a smile to match her own, but instead he finds himself flinging his dirty towels at her feet and snapping: 'These towels are damp! See to it that they are replaced!' 'Yes, sir!' 'Moreover, your apron strings are dangling untidily and there are flyspecks on the mirror!' 'Sir.' 'And another thing!' He strides over to the bed and tears it apart. 'Isn't it about time these sheets were changed? Or am I supposed to wear them through before they are taken to be washed?' 'But, sir, I just put new—!' 'What? *WHAT*—?!' he storms. 'Answering back to a reproof? Have you forgotten all I've taught you?' 'I – I'm sorry, sir!' 'Never answer back if your master takes occasion to reprove you, except—?' 'Except it be to acknowledge my fault, sir, and that I am sorry for having committed it, promising to amend for the time to come, and to . . . to . . .' 'Am I being unfair?' he insists, unbuckling his belt. 'No, sir,' she says, her eyes downcast, shoulders trembling, her arms pressed tight to her sides.

He is strict but not unkindly. He pays her well, is grateful for her services, treats her respectfully, she doesn't dislike him or even fear him. Nor does she have to work very hard: he is essentially a tidy man, picks up after himself, comes and goes without disturbing things much. A bit of dusting and polishing now and then, fold his pajamas, change the towels, clean the bathroom, scrub the floor, make his bed: really there's nothing to complain about. Yet, vaguely, even as she opens up the garden doors, letting the late morning sunshine and freshness in, she feels unhappy. Not because of what she must do – no, she truly serves with gladness. When she straightens a room, polishes a floor, bleaches a sheet or scrubs a tub, always doing the very best she can, she becomes, she knows, a part of what is good in the world, creating a kind of beauty, revealing a kind of truth. About herself, about life, the things she touches. It's just that, somehow, something is missing. Some response, some enrichment, some direction . . . it's, well, it's too repetitive. Something like that. That's part of the problem anyway. The other part is what she keeps finding in his bed. Things that oughtn't to be there, like old razor blades, broken bottles, banana skins, bloody pessaries, crumbs and ants, leather thongs, mirrors, empty books, old toys, dark stains. Once, even, a frog jumped out at her. No matter how much sunlight and fresh air she lets in, there's always this dark little pocket of lingering night which she has to uncover. It can ruin everything, all her careful preparations. This morning, however, all she finds is a pair of flannelette drawers. Ah: she recognizes them. She glances about guiltily, pulls them on hastily. Lucky the master's in the bathroom, she thinks, patting down her skirt and apron, or there'd be the devil to pay.

Something about scouring, or scourging, he can't remember, and a teacher he once had who called his lectures 'lechers.' The maid is standing over him, staring down in some astonishment at his erection. 'Oh! I beg your pardon, sir!' 'I was having a dream . . .,' he explains, trying to bring it back. 'Something about a woman . . .' But by then he is alone again. He hears her in the bathroom, running water, singing, whipping the wet towels off the racks and tossing them out the door. Ah well, it's easy for her, she can come and go. He sits up, squinting in the bright light, watching his erection dip back inside his pajamas like a sleeper pulling the blankets over his head (oh yes! to return there!), then dutifully shoves his feet into slippers, stretches, staggers to the open garden doors. The air is fragrant and there's a morning racket of birds and insects, vaguely threatening. Sometimes, as now, scratching himself idly and dragging himself still from the stupor of sleep, he wonders about his calling, how it came to be his, and when it all began: on his coming here? on *her* coming here? before that, in some ancient time beyond recall? And has he chosen it? or has he, like that woman in his dream, showing him something that for some reason enraged him, been 'born with it, sir, for your very utility'?

She strives, understanding the futility of it, for perfection. To arrive properly equipped, to cross the room deliberately, circumspectly, without affectation (as he has taught her), to fling open the garden doors and let the sweet breath of morning flow in and chase the night away, to strip and air the bed and, after all her common tasks, her trivial round, to remake it smooth and tight, all the sheets and blankets tucked in neatly at the sides and bottom, the upper sheet and blankets turned down at the head just so far that their fold covers only half the pillows, all topped with the spread, laid to hang evenly at all sides. And today – perhaps at last! She straightens up, wipes her brow, looks around: yes! he'll be so surprised! Everything perfect! Her heart is pounding as the master, dressed for the day, steps out of the bathroom, marches directly over to the bed, hauls back the covers, picks up a pillow, and hits her in the face with it. Now what did he do that for? 'And another thing!' he says.

He awakes, feeling sorry for himself (he's not sure why, something he's been dreaming perhaps, or merely the need to wake just by itself: come, day, do your damage!), tears himself painfully from the bed's embrace, sits up, pushes his feet into slippers. He grunts, squinting in the dimness at his watch: she's late. Just as well. He can shower before she gets here. He staggers into the bathroom and drops his pajamas, struggling to recall his dream. Something about a woman in the civil service, which in her ignorance or cupidity, she insisted on calling the 'sibyl service.' He is relieving himself noisily when the maid comes in. 'Oh! I beg your pardon, sir!' 'Good morning,' he replies crisply, and pulls his pajamas up, but she is gone. He can hear her outside the door, walking quickly back and forth, flinging open the curtains and garden doors, singing to herself as though lifted by the tasks before her. Sometimes he envies her, having him. Her footsteps carry her to the bed and he hears the rush and flutter of sheets and blankets being thrown back. Hears her scream.

He's not unkind, demands no more than is his right, pays her well, and teaches her things like, 'All life is a service, a consecration to some high end,' and, 'If domestic service is to be tolerable, there must be an attitude of habitual deference on the one side and one of sympathetic protection on the other.' 'Every state and condition of life has its particular duties,' he has taught her. 'The duty of a servant is to be obedient, diligent, sober, just, honest, frugal, orderly in her behavior, submissive and respectful toward her master. She must be contented in her station, because it is necessary that some should be above others in this world, and it was the will of the Almighty to place you in a state of servitude.' Her soul, in short, is his invention, and she is grateful to him for it. '*Whatever thy hand findeth to do,*' he has admonished, '*do it with all thy might!*' Nevertheless, looking over her shoulder at her striped sit-me-down in the wardrobe mirror, she wishes he might be a little less literal in applying his own maxims: *he's drawn blood!*

He awakes, mumbling something about a dream, a teacher he once had, some woman, infirmities. 'A sort of fever of the mind,' he explains, his throat phlegmy with sleep. 'Yes, sir,' she says, and flings open the curtains and the garden doors, letting light and air into the stale bedroom. She takes pleasure in all her appointed tasks, but enjoys this one most of all, more so when the master is already out of bed, for he seems to resent her waking him like this. Just as he resents her arriving late, after he's risen. Either way, sooner or later, she'll have to pay for it. 'It's a beautiful day,' she remarks hopefully. He sits up with an ambiguous grunt, rubs his eyes, yawns, shudders. 'You may speak when spoken to,' he grumbles, tucking his closing morning glory back inside his pajamas (behind her, bees are humming in the garden and there's a crackly pulsing of insects, but the birds have fallen silent: she had thought today might be perfect, but already it is slipping away from her), 'unless it be to deliver a message or ask a necessary question.' 'Yes, sir.' He shoves his feet into slippers and staggers off to the bathroom, leaving her to face (she expects the worst) – shadows have invaded the room – the rumpled bed alone.

It's not just the damp towels. It's also the streaked floor, the careless banging of the garden doors, her bedraggled uniform, the wrinkled sheets, the confusion of her mind. He lectures her patiently on the proper way to make a bed, the airing of the blankets, turning of the mattress, changing of the sheets, the importance of a smooth surface. 'Like a blank sheet of crisp new paper,' he tells her. He shows her how to make the correct diagonal creases at the corners, how to fold the top edge of the upper sheet back over the blankets, how to carry the spread under and then over the pillows. Oh, not for his benefit and advantage – he could sleep anywhere or for that matter (in extremity) could make his own bed – but for hers. How else would she ever be able to realize what is best in herself? 'A little arrangement and thought will give you method and habit,' he explains (it is his 'two fairies' lecture), but though she seems willing enough, is polite and deferential, even eager to please, she can never seem to get it just right. Is it a weakness on her part, he wonders as he watches her place the pillows on the bed upside down, then tug so hard on the bottom blanket that it comes out at the foot, or some perversity? Is she testing him? She refits the bottom blanket, tucks it in again, but he knows the sheet beneath is now wrinkled. He sighs, removes his belt. Perfection is elusive, but what else is there worth striving for? 'Am I being unfair?' he insists.

He's standing there in the sunlight in his slippers and pajama bottoms, cracking his palm with a leather strap, when she enters (once and for all) with all her paraphernalia. She plants the bucket and brushes beside the door, leans the mop and broom against the wall, stacks the fresh linens and towels on a chair. She is late – the curtains and doors are open, her circumspect crossing of the room no longer required – but she remains hopeful. Running his maxims over in her head, she checks off her rags and brushes, her polishes, cleaning powders, razor blades, toilet paper, dust-pans – oh no . . .! Her heart sinks like soap in a bucket. The soap she has forgotten to bring. She sighs, then deliberately and gravely, without affectation, not stamping too loud, nor dragging her legs after her, not marching as if leading a dance, nor keeping time with her head and hands, nor staring or turning her head either one way or the other, she advances sedately and discreetly across the gleaming tiles to the bed, and tuck-ing up her dress and apron, pulling down her flannelette drawers, bends over the foot of it, exposing her soul's ingress to the sweet breath of morning, blowing in from the garden. 'I wonder if you can appreciate,' he says, picking a bit of lint off his target before applying his corrective measures to it, 'how difficult this is for me?'

He awakes, vaguely frightened by something he has dreamt (it was about order or odor and a changed condition – but how did it begin . . . ?), wound up in damp sheets and unable at first even to move, defenseless against the day already hard upon him. Its glare blinds him, but he can hear the maid moving about the room, sweeping the floor, changing the towels, running water, pushing furniture around. 'Good morning, sir,' she says. 'Come here a moment,' he replies gruffly, then clears his throat. 'Sir?' 'Look under the bed. Tell me what you see.' He expects the worst: blood, a decapitated head, a bottomless hole . . . 'I'm – I'm sorry, sir,' she says, tucking up her skirt and apron, lowering her drawers, 'I thought I *had* swept it . . .'

No matter how much fresh air and sunlight she lets in, there is always this little pocket of lingering night which she has to uncover. Once she found a dried bull's pizzle in there, another time a dead mouse in a trap. Even the nice things she finds in the bed are somehow horrible: the toys broken, the food moldy, the clothing torn and bloody. She knows she must always be circumspect and self-effacing, never letting her countenance betray the least dislike toward any task, however trivial or distasteful, and she resolves every morning to be cheerful and good-natured, letting nothing she finds there put her out of temper with everything besides, but sometimes she cannot help herself. 'Oh, teach me, my God and King, in all things thee to see, and what I do in any thing, to do it as for thee,' she tells herself, seeking courage, and flings back the sheets and blankets. She screams. But it's only money, a little pile of gold coins, agleam with promise. Or challenge: is he testing her?

Oh well, he envies her, even as that seat chosen by Mother Nature for such interventions quivers and reddens under the whistling strokes of the birch rod in his hand. 'Again!' 'Be ... be diligent in endeavoring to please your master – be faithful and ... and ...' Swish-*SNAP!* 'Oh, sir!' 'Honest!'

'Yes, sir!' She, after all, is free to come and go, her correction finitely inscribed by time and the manuals, but he . . . He sighs unhappily. How did it all begin, he wonders. Was it destiny, choice, generosity? If she would only get it right for once, he reasons, bringing his stout engine of duty down with a sharp report on her brightly striped but seemingly unimpressionable hinder parts, he might at least have time for a stroll in the garden. Does she – *CRACK!* – think he enjoys this? 'Well?' 'Be . . . be faithful, honest and submissive to him, sir, and—' Whish-*SLASH!* 'And – *gasp!* – do not incline to be slothful! Or—' *THWOCK!* 'Ow! Please, sir!' Hiss-*WHAP!* She groans, quivers, starts. The two raised hemispheres upon which the blows from the birch rod have fallen begin (predictably) to make involuntary motions both vertically and horizontally, the constrictor muscle being hard at work, the thighs also participating in the general vibrations, all in all a dismal spectacle. And for nothing? So it would seem . . . 'Or?' 'Or lie long in bed, sir, but rise . . . rise early in a morning!' The weals crisscross each other on her enflamed posteriors like branches against the pink clouds of dawn, which for some reason saddens

him. 'Am I being unfair?' 'No – no, s—' Whisp-
CRACK! She shows no tears, but her face pressed
against the bedding is flushed, her lips trembling,
and she breathes heavily as though she's been
running, confirming the quality of the rod which
is his own construction. 'Sir,' he reminds her,
turning away. 'Sir,' she replies faintly. 'Thank
you, sir.'

She enters, once and for all, radiant and clear-
browed (a long devotion to duty), with all her
paraphernalia, her mop and bucket, brooms, rags,
soaps, polishes, sets them all down, counting them
off on her fingers, then crosses the room deliberately and circumspectly, not glancing at the
rumpled bed, and flings open the curtains and the
garden doors to call forth the morning, what's left
of it. There is such a song of insects all about (the
preying birds are silent) – what inspiration! 'Lord,
keep me in my place!' The master is in the shower:
she hears the water. 'Let me be diligent in per-
forming whatever my master commands me,' she
prays, 'neat and clean in my habit, modest in my
carriage, silent when he is angry, willing to please,

quick and neat-handed about what I do, and always
of an humble and good disposition!' Then, excited
to the most generous and efficient accomplishments, she turns with a palpitating heart (she is
thinking about perfect service and freedom and
the unpleasant things she has found) to the opening up and airing of the bed. She braces herself,
expecting the worst, but finds only a wilted flower
from the garden: ah! today then! she thinks hopefully – perhaps at last! But then she hears the
master turn the taps off, step out of the shower.
Oh no . . . ! She lowers her drawers to her knees,
lifts her dress, and bends over the unmade bed.
'These towels are damp!' he blusters, storming out
of the bathroom, wielding the fearsome rod, that
stout engine of duty, still wet from the shower.

Sometimes he uses a rod, sometimes his hand, his
belt, sometimes a whip, a cane, a cat-o'-nine-
tails, a bull's pizzle, a hickory switch, a martinet,
ruler, slipper, a leather strap, a hairbrush. There
are manuals for this. Different preparations and
positions to be assumed, the number and severity
of the strokes generally prescribed to fit the of-

fense, he has explained it all to her, though it is not what is important to her. She knows he is just, could not be otherwise if he tried, even if the relative seriousness of the various infractions seems somewhat obscure to her at times. No, what matters to her is the idea behind the regulations that her daily tasks, however trivial, are perfectible. Not absolutely perhaps, but at least in terms of the manuals. This idea, which is almost tangible – made manifest, as it were, in the weals on her behind – is what the punishment is for, she assumes. She does not enjoy it certainly, nor (she believes – and it wouldn't matter if he did) does he. Rather, it is a road (speaking loosely), the rod, to bring her daily nearer God – and what's more, it seems that she's succeeding at last! Today everything has been perfect: her entry, all her vital paraphernalia, her circumspect crossing of the room and opening of the garden doors, her scrubbing and waxing and dusting and polishing, her opening up and airing and making of the master's bed – everything! True service, she knows (he has taught her!), is perfect freedom, and today she feels it: almost like a breeze – the sweet breath of success – lifting her! But then the master emerges from the bathroom, his hair wild, fumbles through the clothes hanging in the wardrobe, pokes through the dresser drawers, whips back the covers of her perfectly made bed. 'What's this doing here –?!' he demands, holding up his comb. 'I – I'm sorry, sir! It wasn't there when I—' 'What? *What –?!*' He seizes her by the elbow, drags her to the foot of the bed, forces her to bend over it. 'I have been very indulgent to you up to now, but now I am going to punish you severely, to cure you of your insolent clumsiness once and for all! So pull up your skirt – come! pull it up! you know well enough that the least show of resistance means ten extra cuts of the – *what's this—?!*' She peers round her shoulder at her elevated sit-me-down, so sad and pale above her stockings. 'I – I don't understand, sir! I had them on when I came in—!'

Perhaps he's been pushing her too hard, he muses, soaping himself in the shower and trying to recall the dream he was having when she woke him up (something about ledgers and manual positions, a woman, and the merciless invention of souls which was a sort of fever of the mind), perhaps he's been expecting too much too soon, making her overanxious, for in some particulars now she is almost too efficient, clattering in with her paraphernalia like a soldier, blinding him with a sudden brutal flood of sunlight from the garden, hauling the sheets out from under him while he's still trying to stuff his feet into his slippers. Perhaps he should back off a bit, give her a chance to recover some of her ease and spontaneity, even at the expense of a few undisciplined errors. Perhaps . . . yet he knows he could never let up, even if he tried. Not that he enjoys all this punishment, any more (he assumes, but it doesn't matter) than she does. No, he would rather do just about anything else – crawl back into bed, read his manuals, even take a stroll in the garden – but he is committed to a higher end, his life a mission of sorts, a consecration, and so punish her he must, for to the extent that she fails, he fails. As he turns off the taps and steps out of the shower, reaching for the towel, the maid rushes in. 'Oh, I beg your pardon, sir!' He grabs a towel and wraps it around him, but she snatches it away again: 'That one's damp, sir!' She dashes out to fetch him a fresh one and he is moved by her transparent enthusiasm, her eagerness to please, her seemingly unquenchable appetite for hope: perhaps today ...! But he has already noticed that she has forgotten her lace cap, there's a dark stain on the bib of her apron, and her garters are dangling. He sighs, reaches for the leather strap. Somehow (is there to be no end to this? he wonders ruefully) it should be easier than this.

She does not enjoy the discipline of the rod, nor does he – or so he believes, though what would it matter if he did? Rather, they are both dedicated to the fundamental proposition (she winces at the painful but unintended pun, while peering over her shoulder at herself in the wardrobe mirror, tracing the weals with her fingertips) that her daily tasks, however trivial, are perfectible, her punishments serving her as a road, loosely speaking, to bring her daily nearer God, at least in terms of the manuals. Tenderly, she lifts her drawers up over her blistered sit-me-down, smoothes down her black alpaca dress and white lace apron, wipes the tears from her eyes, and turns once more to the unmade bed. Outside, the bees humming in the noonday sun remind her of all the time she has lost. At least, she consoles herself, the worst is past. But the master is pacing the room impatiently and she's fearful his restlessness will confuse her again. 'Why don't you go for a stroll in the garden, sir?' she suggests deferentially. 'You may speak when spoken to!' he reminds her, jabbing a finger at her sharply. 'I – I'm sorry, sir!' 'You must be careful not only to do your work quietly, but to keep out of sight as much as possible, and never begin to speak to your master unless—?' 'Unless it be to deliver a message, sir, or ask a necessary question!' 'And then to do it in as few words as possible,' he adds, getting down his riding whip. 'Am I being unfair?' 'But, sir! you've already— !' 'What? *What*—?! Answering back to a reproof—?' 'But— !' '*Enough!*' he rages, seizing her by the arm and dragging her over to the bed. '*Please—!*' But he pulls her down over his left knee, pushes her head down on the stripped mattress, locking her legs in place with his right leg, clamps her right wrist in the small of her back, throws her skirts back and jerks her drawers down. '*Oh, sir—!*' she pleads, what is now her highest part still radiant and throbbing from the previous lesson.

'SILENCE!' he roars, lifting the whip high above his head, a curious strained expression on his face. She can hear the whip sing as he brings it down, her cheeks pinch together involuntarily, her heart leaps – *he'll draw blood!*

Where does she come from? Where does she go? He doesn't know. All he knows is that every day she comes here, dressed in her uniform and carrying all her paraphernalia with her, which she sets down by the door; then she crosses the room, opens up the curtains and garden doors, makes his bed soft and easy, first airing the bedding, turning the mattress, and changing the linens, scrubs and waxes the tiled floor, cleans the bathroom, polishes the furniture and all the mirrors, replenishes all supplies, and somewhere along the way commits some fundamental blunder, obliging him to administer the proper correction. Every day the same. Why does he persist? It's not so much that he shares her appetite for hope (though sometimes, late in the day, he does), but that he could not do otherwise should he wish. To live in the full sense of the word, he knows, is not merely to exist, but to give oneself to some mission, surrender to a higher purpose, but in truth he often wonders, watching that broad part destined by Mother Nature for such solemnities quiver and redden under his hand (he thinks of it as a blank ledger on which to write), whether it is he who has given himself to a higher end, or that end which has chosen and in effect captured him?

Perhaps, she thinks, I'd better go out and come in again . . . And so she enters. As though once and for all, though she's aware she can never be sure of this. She sets down beside the door all the vital paraphernalia of her office, checking off each item on her fingers, then crosses the room (circumspectly etc.) and flings open the curtains and garden doors to the midday sun. Such a silence all about? She tries to take heart from it, but it is not so inspiring as the song of birds, and even the bees seem to have ceased their humming. Though she has resolved, as always, to be cheerful and goodnatured, truly serving with gladness as she does, she nevertheless finds her will flagging, her mind clouded with old obscurities: somehow, something is missing. 'Teach me, my God and King, in all things thee to see,' she recites dutifully, but the words seem meaningless to her and go nowhere. And now, once again, the hard part. She holds back, trembling – but what can she do about it? For she knows her place and is contented with her station, as he has taught her. She takes a deep breath of the clean warm air blowing in from the garden and, fearing the worst, turns upon the bed, hurls the covers back, and screams. But it is only the master. 'Oh! I beg your pardon, sir!' 'A . . . a dream,' he explains huskily, as his erection withdraws into his pajamas like a worm caught out in the sun, burrowing for shade. 'Something about a lecture on civil severity, what's left of it, and an inventory of soaps . . . or hopes . . .' He's often like that as he struggles (never very willingly, it seems to her) out of sleep. She leaves him there, sitting on the edge of the bed, squinting in the bright light, yawning and scratching himself and muttering something depressing about being born again, and goes to the bathroom to change the towels, check the toothpaste and toilet paper, wipe the mirror and toilet seat, and put fresh soap in the shower tray, doing the will of God and the manuals, endeavoring to please. As he shuffles groggily in, already reaching inside his fly, she slips out, careful not to speak as she's not been spoken to, and returns to the rumpled bed. She tosses back the blankets afresh (nothing new, thank you, sir), strips away the soiled linens, turns and brushes the mattress (else it might imbibe an unhealthy kind of dampness and become unpleasant), shakes the feather pillows and sets everything out to air. While the master showers, she dusts the furniture, polishes the mirrors, and mops the floor, then remakes the bed, smooth and tight, all the sheets and blankets tucked in neatly at the sides and bottom, the top sheet turned down at the head, over the blankets, the spread carried under, then over the pillows, and hanging equally low at both sides and the foot: ah! it's almost an act of magic! But are those flyspecks on the mirror? She rubs the mirror, and seeing herself reflected there, thinks to check that her apron strings are tied and her stocking seams are straight. Peering over her shoulder at herself, her eye falls on the mirrored bed: one of the sheets is dangling at the foot, peeking out from under the spread as though exposing itself rudely. She hurries over, tucks it in, being careful to make the proper diagonal fold, but now the spread seems to be hanging lower on one side than the other. She whips it back, dragging the top sheet and blankets part way with it. The taps have been turned off, the master is drying himself. Carefully, she remakes the bed, tucking in all the sheets and blankets properly, fluffing the pillows up once more, covering it all with the spread, hung evenly. All this bedmaking has raised a lot of dust: she can see her own tracks on the floor. Hurriedly she wipes the furniture again and sweeps the tiles. Has she bumped the bed somehow? The spread is askew once again like a gift coming unwrapped. She tugs it to one side, sees ripples appear on top. She tries to smooth them down, but apparently the blankets are wrinkled underneath. She hasn't pushed the dresser back against the wall. The wardrobe door is open, reflecting the master standing in the doorway to the bathroom, slapping his palm with a bull's pizzle. She stands there, downcast, shoulders trembling, her arms pressed to her sides, unable to move. It's like some kind of failure of communication, she thinks, her diligent endeavors to please him forever thwarted by her irremediable clumsiness. 'Come, come! A little arrangement and thought will give you method and habit,' he reminds her gravely, 'two fairies that will make the work disappear before a ready pair of hands!' In her mind she doesn't quite believe it, but her heart is ever hopeful, her hands readier than he knows. She takes the bed apart once more and remakes it from the beginning, tucking everything in correctly, fluffing the pillows, laying the spread evenly: all tight and smooth it looks. Yes! She pushes the dresser (once he horsed her there: she shudders to recall it, a flush of dread racing through her) back against the wall, collects the wet towels he has thrown on the floor, closes the wardrobe door. In the mirror, she sees the bed. The spread and blankets have been thrown back, the sheets pulled out. In the bathroom doorway, the master taps his palm with the stretched-out bull's pizzle, testing its firmness and elasticity, which she knows to be terrifying in its perfection. She remakes the bed tight and smooth, not knowing what else to do, vaguely aware as she finishes of an unpleasant odor. Under the bed? Also her apron is missing and she seems to have a sheet left over. Shadows creep across the room, silent now but for the rhythmic tapping of the pizzle in the master's hand and the pounding of her own palpitating heart.

Sometimes he stretches her across his lap. Sometimes she must bend over a chair or the bed, or lie flat out on it, or be horsed over the pillows, the dresser or a stool, there are manuals for this. Likewise her drawers: whether they are to be drawn tight over her buttocks like a second skin or lowered, and if lowered, by which of them, how far, and so on. Her responses are assumed in the texts (the writhing, sobbing, convulsive quivering, blushing, moaning, etc.), but not specified, except insofar as they determine his own further reactions – to resistance, for example, or premature acquiescence, fainting, improper language, an unclean bottom, and the like. Thus, once again, her relative freedom: her striped buttocks tremble and dance spontaneously under the whip which his hand must bring whistling down on them according to canon – ah well, it's not so much that he envies her (her small freedoms cost her something, he knows that), but that he is saddened by her inability to understand how difficult it is for him, and without that understanding it's as though something is always missing, no matter how faithfully he adheres to the regulations. 'And— ?' 'And be neat and clean in your—' whisp-*CRACK!* '– OW! habit! Oh! and wash yourself all over once a day to avoid bad smells and—' hiss-*SNAP!* '– and – *gasp!* – wear strong decent underclothing!' The whip sings a final time, smacks its broad target with a loud report, and little drops of blood appear like punctuation, gratitude, morning dew. 'That will do, then. See that you don't forget to wear them again!' 'Yes, sir.' She lowers her black alpaca skirt gingerly over the glowing crimson flesh as though hooding a lamp, wincing at each touch. 'Thank you, sir.'

For a long time she struggled to perform her tasks in such a way as to avoid the thrashings. But now, with time, she has come to understand that the tasks, truly common, are only peripheral details in some larger scheme of things which includes her punishment – indeed, perhaps depends upon it. Of course she still performs her duties *as though* they were perfectible and her punishment could be avoided, ever diligent in endeavoring to please him who guides her, but though each day the pain surprises her afresh, the singing of the descending instrument does not. That God has ordained bodily punishment (and Mother Nature designed the proper place of martyrdom) is beyond doubt – every animal is governed by it, understands and fears it, and the fear of it keeps every creature in its own sphere, forever preventing (as he has taught her) that natural confusion and disorder that would instantly arise without it. Every state and condition of life has its particular duties, and each is subject to the divine government of pain, nothing could be more obvious, and looked on this way, his chastisements are not merely necessary, they might even be beautiful. Or so she consoles herself, trying to take heart, calm her rising panic, as she crosses the room under his stern implacable gaze, lowers her drawers as far as her knees, tucks her skirt up, and bends over the back of a chair, hands on the seat, thighs taut and pressed closely together, what is now her highest part tensing involuntarily as though to reduce the area of pain, if not the severity. 'It's . . . it's a

beautiful day, sir,' she says hopefully. 'What?
WHAT— ?!'

Relieving himself noisily in the bathroom, the
maid's daily recitals in the next room (such a blast
of light out there – even in here he keeps his eyes
half closed) thus drowned out, he wonders if
there's any point in going on. She is late, has
left half her paraphernalia behind, is improperly
dressed, and he knows, even without looking, that
the towels are damp. Maybe it's some kind of
failure of communication. A mutual failure. Is that
possible? A loss of syntax between stroke and weal?
No, no, even if possible, it is unthinkable. He turns
on the shower taps and lets fall his pajama pants,
just as the maid comes in with a dead fetus and
drops it down the toilet, flushes it. 'I found it in
your bed, sir,' she explains gratuitously (is she
testing him?), snatching up the damp towels, but
failing to replace them with fresh ones. At least
she's remembered her drawers today: she's wearing
them around her ankles. He sighs as she shuffles
out. Maybe he should simply forget it, go for a

stroll in the garden or something, crawl back into bed (a dream, he recalls now: something about lectures or ledgers – an inventory perhaps – and a bottomless hole, glass breaking, a woman doing what she called 'the hard part' . . . or did she say 'heart part'?), but of course he cannot, even if he truly wished to. He is not a free man, his life is consecrated, for though he is *her* master, her failures are inescapably *his*. He turns off the shower taps, pulls up his pajama pants, takes down the six-thonged martinet. 'I have been very indulgent to you up to now,' he announces, stepping out of the bathroom, 'but now I am going to punish you severely, so pull up your skirt, come! pull it up!' But, alas, it is already up. She is bent over the foot of the bed, her pale hinder parts already exposed for his ministrations, an act of insolence not precisely covered by his manuals. Well, he reasons wryly, making the martinet sing whole chords, if improvisation is denied him, interpretation is not. 'Ow, sir! Please! *You'll draw blood, sir!*'

'Neat and clean in habit, modest—' *WHACK!* '– . . . in carriage, silent when—' Whisp-*SNAP!* 'OW!!'

'Be careful! If you move, the earlier blow won't count!' 'I – I'm sorry, sir!' Her soul, she knows, is his invention, and she is grateful to him for it, but exposed like this to the whining slashes of the cane and the sweet breath of mid-afternoon which should cool his righteous ardor but doesn't (once a bee flew in and stung him on the hand: what did it mean? nothing: she got it on her sit-me-down once, too, and he took the swelling for a target), her thighs shackled by flannelette drawers and blood rushing to her head, she can never remember (for all the times he has explained it to her) why it is that Mother Nature has chosen that particular part of her for such solemnities: it seems more like a place for lettings things out than putting things in. 'Well? Silent when—?' 'Silent when he is angry, willing to please, quick and—' swish-*CRACK!* '– and of good disposition!' 'Sir,' he reminds her: *THWOCK!* 'SIR!' she cries. 'Very well, but you must learn to take more pleasure in your appointed tasks, however trivial or unpleasant, and when you are ordered to do anything, do not grumble or let your countenance betray any dislike thereunto, but do it cheerfully and readily!' 'Yes, sir! Thank you, sir!' She is all hot behind, and peering over her

shoulder at herself in the wardrobe mirror after the
master has gone to shower, she can see through her
tears that it's like on fire, flaming crimson it is, with
large blistery welts rising and throbbing like things
alive: he's drawn blood! She dabs at it with her
drawers, recalling a dream he once related to her
about a teacher he'd had who called his chastisements
'scripture lessons,' and she understands now what
he's always meant by demanding 'a clean sheet of
paper.' Well, certainly it has always been clean, neat
and clean as he's taught her, that's one thing she's
never got wrong, always washing it well every day
in three hot lathers, letting the last lather be made
thin of the soap, then not rinsing it or toweling it,
but drying it over brimstone, keeping it as much
from the air as possible, for that, she knows, will
spoil it if it comes to it. She finishes drying it by
slapping it together in her hands, then holding it
before a good fire until it be thoroughly hot, then
clapping it and rubbing it between her hands from
the fire, occasionally adding to its fairness by giving
it a final wash in a liquor made of rosemary flowers
boiled in white wine. Now, she reasons, lifting her
drawers up gingerly over the hot tender flesh, which
is still twitching convulsively, if she could just apply

those same two fairies, method and habit, to the
rest of her appointed tasks, she might yet find in
them that pleasure he insists she take, according to
the manuals. Well, anyway, the worst is past. Or so
she consoles herself, as smoothing down her black
skirt and white lace apron, she turns to the bed. *'Oh,
teach me, my God and King, in all things thee to . . .'*
What—? There's something under there! *And it's
moving . . . !*

'Thank you, sir.' 'I know that perfection is elusive,'
he explains, putting away his stout engine of duty,
while she staggers over, her knees bound by her
drawers, to examine her backside in the wardrobe mirror (it is well cut, he knows, and so aglow
one might cook little birds over it or roast chestnuts, as the manuals suggest), 'but what else is
there worth striving for?' 'Yes, sir.' She shows no
tears, but her face is flushed, her lips are trembling,
and she breathes as though she has been running. He goes to gaze out into the garden, vaguely
dissatisfied. The room is clean, the bed stripped
and made, the maid whipped, why isn't that
enough? Is there something missing in the

manuals? No, more likely, he has failed somehow
to read them rightly. Yet again. Outside in the
sleepy afternoon heat of the garden, the bees are
humming, insects chattering, gentler sounds to
be sure than the hiss of a birch rod, the sharp
report as it smacks firm resonant flesh, yet
strangely alien to him, sounds of natural confusion
and disorder from a world without precept or
invention. He sighs. Though he was thinking
'invention,' what he has heard in his inner ear was
'intention,' and now he's not sure which it was he
truly meant. Perhaps he should back off a bit – or
even let her off altogether for a few days. A kind
of holiday from the divine government of pain.
Certainly he does not enjoy it nor (presumably)
does she. If he could ever believe in her as she
believes in him, he might even change places with
her for awhile, just to ease his own burden and
let her understand how difficult it is for him. A
preposterous idea of course, pernicious in fact,
an unthinkable betrayal . . . yet sometimes, late
in the day, something almost like a kind of fever
of the mind (speaking loosely) steals over –
enough! *enough!* no shrinking! 'And another thing!'
he shouts, turning on the bed (she is at the door,

gathering up her paraphernalia) and throwing back the covers: at the foot on the clean crisp sheets there is a little pile of wriggling worms, still coated with dirt from the garden. 'WHAT DOES THIS MEAN—?!' he screams. 'I – I'm sorry, sir! I'll clean it up right away, sir!' Is she testing him? Taunting him? It's almost an act of madness! 'Am I being unfair?' 'But, sir, you've already—!' 'What? *WHAT*—?! Is there to be no *end* to this—?!'

He holds her over his left knee, her legs locked between his, wrist clamped in the small of her back, her skirt up and her drawers down, and slaps her with his bare hand, first one buttock, reddening it smartly in contrast to the dazzling alabaster (remembering the manuals) of the other, then attacking its companion with equal alacrity. 'Ow! Please, sir!' 'Come, come, you know that the least show of resistance means ten extra cuts of the rod!' he admonishes her, doubling her over a chair. 'When you are ordered to do anything, do not grumble or let your countenance betray any dislike thereunto, but do it cheerfully and generously!' 'Yes, sir, but—'

'What? WHAT—?!' Whish-*CRACK!* 'OW!' *SLASH!*
Her crimson bottom, hugged close to the pillows,
bobs and dances under the whistling cane. 'When
anyone finds fault with you, do not answer rudely!'
Whirr-*SMACK!* 'NO, SIR!' Each stroke, surprising her afresh, makes her jerk with pain and wrings
a little cry from her (as anticipated by the manuals
when the bull's pizzle is employed), which she
attempts to stifle by burying her face in the horsehair
cushion. 'Be respectful—?' 'Be respectful and
obedient, sir, to those—' swish-*THWOCK!* '– placed
– OW! – placed OVER you – AARGH!' Whizz-
SWACK! 'With fear and trembling—' *SMASH!* '–
and in singleness of your heart!' he reminds her
gravely as she groans, starts, quivers under his
patient instruction. 'Ouch! Yes, sir!' The leather
strap whistles down to land with a loud crack across
the center of her glowing buttocks, seeming almost
to explode, and making what lilies there are left into
roses. *SMACK!* Ker-*WHACK!* He's working well
now. 'Am I being unfair?' 'N-no, sir!' *WHAP! SLAP!*
Horsed over the dresser her limbs launch out
helplessly with each blow, *'Kneel down!'* She falls
humbly to her hands and knees, her head bowed
between his slippered feet, that broad part destined

by Mother Nature for such devotions elevated but pointed away from him toward the wardrobe mirror (as though trying, flushed and puffed up, to cry out to itself), giving him full and immediate access to that large division referred to in the texts as the Paphian grove. 'And resolve every morning –?' 'Resolve – *gasp!* – resolve every morning to be cheerful and—' He raises the whip, snaps it three times around his head, and brings it down with a crash on her hinder parts, driving her head forward between his legs. 'And – *YOW!* – and good-natured that ... that day, and if any ... if any accident – *groan!* – should happen to –' swish-*WHACK!* '– to break that resolution, suffer it ... suffer it not—' *SLASH!* 'Oh, sir!' *SWOCK!* He's pushing himself, too, hard perhaps, but he can't – 'Please, sir! *PLEASE!*' She is clinging to his knee, sobbing into his pajama pants, the two raised hemispheres upon which the strokes have fallen making involuntary motions both vertically and horizontally as though sending a message of distress, all the skin wrinkling like the surface of a lake rippled by the wind. 'What are you doing?! *WHAT DOES THIS MEAN—?!*' He spanks her with a hairbrush, lashes her with a cat-o'-nine-tails, flagellates her with nettles, not shrinking from the hard service to be done, this divine drudgery, clear-browed in his devotion to duty. Perhaps today . . . ! 'SIR!' He pauses, breathing heavily. His arm hurts. There is a curious strained expression on her face, flushed like her behind and wet with tears. 'Sir, if you . . . if you don't stop—' 'What? *WHAT*—?!' 'You – you won't know what to do *next!*' 'Ah.' He has just been smacking her with a wet towel, and the damp rush and pop, still echoing in his inner ear, reminds him dimly of a dream, perhaps the one she interrupted when she arrived. In it there was something about humidity, but it kept getting mixed up somehow with hymnody, such that every time she opened her mouth (there was a woman in the dream) damp chords flowed out and stained his ledgers, bleached white as clean sheets. 'I'm so old,' he says, letting his arm drop, 'and still each day . . .' 'Sir?' 'Nothing. A dream . . .' Where was he? It doesn't matter. 'Why don't you go for a stroll in the garden, sir? It's a beautiful day.' Such impudence: he ignores it. 'It's all right,' he says, draping the blood-flecked towel over his shoulder, scratching himself idly. He yawns. 'The worst is past.'

★

Has he devoted himself to a higher end, he wonders, standing there in the afternoon sunlight in his slippers and pajama bottoms, flexing a cane, testing it, snapping it against his palm, or has he been taken captive by it? Is choice itself an illusion? Or an act of magic? And *is* the worst over, or has it not yet begun? He shudders, yawns, stretches. And the manuals . . .? He is afraid even to ask, takes a few practice strokes with the cane against a horsehair cushion instead. When the riddles and paradoxes of his calling overtake him, wrapping him in momentary darkness, he takes refuge in the purity of technique. The proper stretching of a bull's pizzle, for example, this can occupy him for hours. Or the fabrication of whipping chairs, the index of duties and offenses, the synonymy associated with corporal discipline and with that broad part destined by Mother Nature for such services. And a cane is not simply any cane, but preferably one made like this one of brown Malacca – the stem of an East Indian rattan palm – about two and a half feet long (give or take an inch and a half) and a quarter of an inch thick. Whing-*SNAP!* listen to it! Or take the birch rod, not a mere random handful of birchen twigs, as often supposed, but an instrument of precise and elaborate construction. First, the twigs must be meticulously selected for strength and elasticity, each about two feet long, full of snap and taken from a young tree, the tips sharp as needles. Then carefully combining the thick with the thin and slender, they must be bound together for half their length, tightly enough that they might enjoy long service, yet not too tightly or else the rod will be like a stick and the twigs have no play. The rod must fit conveniently to the hand, have reach and swing so as to sing in the air, the larger part of all punishment being the anticipation of course, not the pain, and must immediately raise welts and blisters, surprising the chastised flesh afresh with each stroke. To be sure, it is easier to construct a birch rod than to employ it correctly – that's always the hard part, he doesn't enjoy it, nor does she surely, but the art of the rod is incomplete without its perfect application. And though elusive, what else is there worth striving for? Indeed, he knows he has been too indulgent toward her up till now, treating her with the civility and kindness due to an inferior, but forgetting the forging of her soul by way of those 'vivid lessons,' as a teacher he once had used to put it, 'in holy scripture, hotly writ.' So when she arrives, staggering in late with all her paraphernalia, her bucket empty and her bib hanging down, he orders her straight to the foot of the bed. 'But, sir, I haven't even—' 'Come, come, no dallying! The least show of resistance will double the punishment! Up with your skirt, up, up! for I intend to – WHAT?! IS THERE TO BE NO END TO THIS—?!' 'I – I'm sorry! I was wearing them when I came – I must have left them somewhere . . .!' Maybe it's some kind of communication problem, he thinks, staring gloomily at her soul's ingress which confronts him like blank paper, laundered tiffany, a perversely empty ledger. The warm afternoon sun blows in through the garden doors, sapping his brave resolve. He feels himself drifting, yawning, must literally shake himself to bring the manuals back to mind, his duties, his devotion . . . 'Sir,' she reminds him. 'Sir,' he sighs.

It never ends. Making the bed, she scatters dust and feathers afresh or tips over the mop bucket. Cleaning up the floor, she somehow disturbs the bed. Or something does. It's almost as if it were

alive. Blankets wrinkle, sheets peek perversely out
from under the spread, pillows seem to sag or puff
up all by themselves if she turns her back, and if
she doesn't, then flyspecks break out on the mirror
behind her like pimples, towels start to drip, stains
appear on her apron. If she hasn't forgotten it. She
sighs, turns once more on the perfidious bed.
Though always of an humble and good disposition
(as she's been taught), diligent in endeavoring to
please him, and grateful for the opportunity to do
the will of God from the heart by serving him (true
service, perfect freedom, she knows all about that),
sometimes, late in the day like this (shadows are
creeping across the room and in the garden the
birds are beginning to sing again), she finds herself
wishing she could make the bed once and for all:
glue down the sheets, sew on the pillows, stiffen
the blankets as hard as boards and nail them into
place. But then what? She cannot imagine. Something frightening. No, no, better this trivial round,
these common tasks, and a few welts on her
humble sit-me-down, she reasons, tucking the
top sheet and blankets in neatly at the sides and
bottom, turning them down at the head just so far
that their fold covers half the pillows, than be

overtaken by confusion and disorder. '*Teach me, my God and King,*' she sings out hopefully, floating the spread out over the bed, allowing it to fall evenly on all sides, '*in all things thee to—*' But then, as the master steps out of the bathroom behind her, she sees the blatant handprints on the wardrobe mirror, the streamers of her lace cap peeking out from under the dresser, standing askew. 'I'm sorry, sir,' she says, bending over the foot of the bed, presenting to him that broad part destined by Mother Nature for the arduous invention of souls. But he ignores it. Instead he tears open the freshly made bed, crawls into it fully dressed, kicking her in the face through the blankets with his shoes, pulls the sheets over his head, and commences to snore. Perhaps, she thinks, her heart sinking, I'd better go out and come in again . . .

Perhaps I should go for a stroll in the garden, he muses, dutifully reddening one resonant cheek with a firm volley of slaps, then the other, according to the manuals. I'm so old, and still . . . He sighs ruefully, recalling a dream he was having when the maid arrived (when was that?), something about a woman, bloody morning glories (or perhaps in the dream they were 'mourning' glories: there was also something about a Paphian grave), and a bee that flew in and stung him on his tumor, which kept getting mixed up somehow with his humor, such that, swollen with pain, he was laughing like a dead man . . . 'Sir?' 'What? *WHAT—?!*' he cries, starting up. 'Ah . . .' His hand is resting idly on her flushed behind as though he meant to leave it there. 'I . . . I was just testing the heat,' he explains gruffly, taking up the birch rod, testing it for strength and elasticity to wake his fingers up. 'When I'm finished, you'll be able to cook little birds over it or roast chestnuts!' He raises the rod, swings it three times round his head, and brings it down with a whirr and a slash, reciting to himself from the manuals to keep his mind, clouded with old obscurities, on the task before him: 'Sometimes the operation is begun a little above the garter—' whish-*SNAP!* '– and ascending the pearly inverted cones –' hiss-*WHACK!* '– is carried by degrees to the dimpled promontories –' *THWOCK!* '– which are vulgarly called the buttocks!' *SMASH!* 'Ow, sir! PLEASE!' She twists about on his knee, biting her lip, her highest part flexing and quivering with each blow, her knees scissoring frantically between his legs. 'Oh, teach me,' she cries out, trying to stifle the sobs, 'my God and—' whizz-*CRACK!* '– King, thee – *gasp!* – to—' *WHAP!* '– SEE!' Sometimes, especially late in the day like this, watching the weals emerge from the blank page of her soul's ingress like secret writing, he finds himself searching it for something, he doesn't know what exactly, a message of sorts, the revelation of a mystery in the spreading flush, in the pout and quiver of her cheeks, the repressed stutter of the little explosions of wind, the – whush-*SMACK!* – dew-bejeweled hieroglyphs of crosshatched stripes. But no, the futility of his labors, that's all there is to read there. Birdsong, no longer threatening, floats in on the warm afternoon breeze while he works. There *was* a bee once, he remembers, that part of his dream was true. Only it stung him on his hand, as though to remind him of the painful burden of his office. For a long time after that he kept the garden doors closed altogether, until he realized one day, spanking the maid for failing to air the bedding properly, that he was in some wise interfering with the manuals. And what has she done wrong today? he wonders, tracing the bloody welts with his

fingertips. He has forgotten. It doesn't matter. He
can lecture her on those two fairies, confusion and
disorder. Method and habit, rather ... 'Sir ...?'
'Yes, yes, in a minute ...' He leans against the
bedpost. To live in the full sense of the word, he
reminds himself, is not to exist or subsist merely,
but to ... to ... He yawns. He doesn't remember.

While examining the dismal spectacle of her
throbbing sit-me-down in the wardrobe mirror (at
least the worst is past, she consoles herself, only
half believing it), a solution of sorts to that problem
of genesis that's been troubling her occurs to her:
to wit, that change (she is thinking about change
now, and conditions) is eternal, has no beginning
– only conditions can begin or end. Who knows,
perhaps he has even taught her that. He has taught
her so many things, she can't be sure anymore.
Everything from habitual deference and the washing of tiffany to pillow fluffing, true service and
perfect freedom, the two fairies that make the
work (speaking loosely) disappear, proper carriage,
sheet folding, and the divine government of pain.
Sometimes, late in the day, or on being awakened,

he even tells her about his dreams, which seem to be mostly about lechers and ordure and tumors and bottomless holes (once he said 'souls'). In a way it's the worst part of her job (that and the things she finds in the bed: today it was broken glass). Once he told her of a dream about a bird with blood in its beak. She asked him, in all deference, if he was afraid of the garden, whereupon he ripped her drawers down, horsed her over a stool, and flogged her so mercilessly she couldn't stand up after, much less sit down. Now she merely says, 'Yes, sir,' but that doesn't always temper the vigor of his disciplinary interventions, as he likes to call them. Such a one for words and all that! Tracing the radiant weals on that broad part of her so destined with her fingertips, she wishes that just once she might hear something more like, 'Well done, thou good and faithful servant, depart in peace!' But then what? When she returned, could it ever be the same? Would he even want her back? No, no, she thinks with a faint shudder, lifting her flannelette drawers up gingerly over soul's well-ruptured ingress (she hopes more has got in than is leaking out), the sweet breath of late afternoon blowing in to remind her of the time

lost, the work yet to be done: no, far better her
appointed tasks, her trivial round and daily act of
contrition, no matter how pitiless the master's
interpretation, than consequences so utterly un-
imaginable. So, inspirited by her unquenchable
appetite for hope and clear-browed devotion to
duty, and running his maxims over in her head, she
sets about doing the will of God from the heart,
scouring the toilet, scrubbing the tiled floor, polishing the furniture and mirrors, checking supplies,
changing the towels. All that remains finally is the
making of the bed. But how can she do that, she
worries, standing there in the afternoon sunlight
with stacks of crisp clean sheets in her arms like
empty ledgers, her virtuous resolve sapped by a
gathering sense of dread as penetrating and aseptic
as ammonia, if the master won't get out of it?

She enters, encumbered with her paraphernalia,
which she deposits by the wall near the door,
crosses the room (circumspectly, precipitately, etc.),
and flings open the garden doors, smashing the
glass, as though once and for all. 'Teach me, my
God and King,' she remarks ruefully (such a sweet

breath of amicable violence all about!), 'in all things
thee to – oh! I beg your pardon, sir!' 'A . . . a dream,'
he stammers, squinting in the glare. He is bound
tightly in the damp sheets, can barely move.
'Something about blood and a . . . a . . . I'm so old,
and still each day—' 'Sir . . .?' He clears his throat.
'Would you look under the bed, please, and tell me
what you see?' 'I – I'm sorry, sir,' she replies,
kneeling down to look, a curious strained expression on her face. With a scream, she disappears.
He awakes, his heart pounding. The maid is staring
down at his erection as though frightened of his
righteous ardor: 'Oh, I beg your pardon, sir!' 'It's
nothing . . . a dream,' he explains, rising like the
pink clouds of dawn. 'Something about . . .' But he
can no longer remember, his mind is a blank sheet.
Anyway, she is no longer listening. He can hear her
moving busily about the room, dusting furniture,
sweeping the floor, changing the towels, taking a
shower. He's standing there abandoned to the
afternoon sunlight in his slippers and pajama
bottoms, which seem to have imbibed an unhealthy
kind of dampness, when a bird comes in and
perches on his erection, what's left of it. 'Ah—!'
'Oh, I beg your pardon, sir!' 'It's – it's nothing,' he

replies hoarsely, blinking up at her, gripped still by claws as fine as waxed threads. 'A dream . . .' But she has left him, gone off singing to her God and King. He tries to pull the blanket back over his head (the bird, its beak opening and closing involuntarily like spanked thighs, was brown as a chestnut, he recalls, and still smoldering, but she returns and snatches it away, the sheets too. Sometimes she can be too efficient. Maybe he has been pushing her too hard, expecting too much too soon. He sits up, feeling rudely exposed (his erection dips back into his pajamas like a frog diving for cover – indeed, it has a greenish cast to it in the half-light of the curtained room: what? isn't she here yet?), and lowers his feet over the side, shuffling dutifully for his slippers. But he can't find them. He can't even find the floor! He jerks back, his skin wrinkling in involuntary panic, but feels the bottom sheet slide out from under him – 'What? *WHAT*—?!' 'Oh, I beg your pardon, sir!' 'Ah . . . it's nothing,' he gasps, struggling to awaken, his heart pounding still (it should be easier than this!), as, screaming, she tucks up her skirt. 'A dream . . .'

★

She enters, as though once and for all, circumspectly deposits her vital paraphernalia beside the door, then crosses the room to fling open (humbly yet authoritatively) the curtains and the garden doors: there is such a song of birds all about! Excited by that, and by the sweet breath of late afternoon, her own eagerness to serve, and faith in the perfectibility of her tasks, she turns with a glad heart and tosses back the bedcovers: 'Oh! I beg your pardon, sir!' 'A . . . a dream,' he mutters gruffly, his erection slipping back inside his pajamas like an abandoned moral. 'Something about glory and a pizzle – or puzzle – and a fundamental position in the civil service . . .' But she is no longer listening, busy now at her common round, dusting furniture and sweeping the floor: so much to do! When (not very willingly, she observes) he leaves the bed at last, she strips the sheets and blankets off, shaking the dead bees into the garden, fluffs and airs the pillows, turns the mattress. She hears the master relieving himself noisily in the bathroom: yes, there's water in the bucket, soap too, a sponge, she's remembered everything! Today then, perhaps at last . . . ! Quickly she polishes the mirror, mops the floor, snaps open the fresh sheets and makes the bed. Before she has the spread down, however, he comes out of the bathroom, staggers across the room muttering something about 'a bloody new birth,' and crawls back into it. 'But, sir—!' 'What, what?' he yawns, and rolls over on his side, pulling the blanket over his head. She snatches it away. He sits up, blinking, a curious strained expression on his face. 'I – I'm sorry, sir,' she says, and, pushing her drawers down to her knees, tucking her skirt up and bending over, she presents to him that broad part preferred by him and Mother Nature for the invention of souls. He retrieves the blanket and disappears under it, all but his feet, which stick out at the bottom, still slippered. She stuffs her drawers hastily behind her apron bib, knocks over the mop bucket, smears the mirror, throws the fresh towels in the toilet, and jerks the blanket away again. 'I – I'm sorry, sir, she insists, bending over and lifting her skirt: 'I'm sure I had them on when I came in . . .' What? Is he snoring? She peers at him past what is now her highest part, that part invaded suddenly by a dread as chilling as his chastisements are, when true to his manuals, enflaming, and realizes with a faint shudder (she cannot hold back the little explosions of wind) that change and condition are coeval and everlasting: a truth as hollow as the absence of birdsong (but they are singing!) . . .

So she stands there in the open doorway, the glass doors having long since been flung open (when was that? she cannot remember), her thighs taut and pressed closely together, her face buried in his cast-off pajamas. She can feel against her cheeks, her lips, the soft consoling warmth of them, so recently relinquished, can smell in them the terror – no, the painful sadness, the divine drudgery (sweet, like crushed flowers, dead birds) – of his dreams, Mother Nature having provided, she knows all too well, the proper place for what God has ordained. But there is another odor in them too, musty, faintly sour, like that of truth or freedom, the fear of which governs every animal, thereby preventing natural confusion and disorder. Or so he has taught her. Now, her face buried in this pungent warmth and her heart sinking, the comforting whirr and smack of his rod no more than a distant echo, disappearing now into the desolate throb of late-afternoon birdsong, she wonders about the manuals, his service to them and hers to him, or to that beyond him which he has not quite named. Whence such an appetite? – she shudders, groans, chewing helplessly on the pajamas – so little relief?

Distantly blows are falling, something about freedom and government, but he is strolling in the garden with a teacher he once had, discussing the condition of humanity, which keeps getting mixed up somehow with homonymity, such that each time his teacher issues a new lament it comes out like slapped laughter. He is about to remark on the generous swish and snap of a morning glory that has sprung up in their path as though inspired ('Paradox, too, has its techniques,' his teacher is saying, 'and so on . . .'), when it turns out to be a woman he once knew on the civil surface. 'What? *WHAT*—?!' But she only wants him to change his position, or perhaps his condition ('You see!' remarks his teacher sagely, unbuckling his belt, 'it's like a kind of callipygomancy, speaking loosely – am I being unfair?'), he's not sure, but anyway it doesn't matter, for what she really wants is to get him out of the sheets he's wrapped in, turn him over (he seems to have imbibed an unhealthy kind of dampness), and give him a lecture (she says 'elixir') on method and fairies, two dew-bejeweled habits you can roast chestnuts over. What more, really, does he want of her? (Perhaps his teacher asks him this, buzzing in and out of his ear like the sweet breath of solemnity: whirr-*SMACK!*) His arm is rising and falling through great elastic spaces as though striving for something fundamental like a forgotten dream or lost drawers. 'I – I'm sorry, sir!' Is she testing him, perched there on his stout engine of duty like a cooked bird with the lingering bucket of night in her beak (see how it opens, closes, opens), or is it only a dimpled fever of the mind? He doesn't know, is almost afraid to ask. 'Something about a higher end,' he explains hoarsely, taking rueful refuge, 'or hired end perhaps, and boiled flowers, hard parts – and another thing, what's left of it . . .' She screams. The garden groans, quivers, starts, its groves radiant and throbbing. His teacher, no longer threatening, has withdrawn discreetly to a far corner with diagonal creases, where he is turning what lilacs remain into roses with his rumpled bull's pizzle: it's almost an act of magic! Still his arm rises and falls, rises and falls, that broad part of Mother Nature destined for such inventions dancing and bobbing soft and easy under the indulgent sun: 'It's a beautiful day!' 'What? *WHAT—?!* An answering back to a reproof?' he inquires gratefully, taunting her with that civility and kindness due to an inferior, as – hiss-*WHAP!* – flicking lint off one shoulder and smoothing the ends of his moustache with involuntary vertical and horizontal motions, he floats helplessly backwards ('Thank you, sir!'), twitching amicably yet authoritatively like a damp towel, down a bottomless hole, relieving himself noisily: '*Perhaps today then . . . at last!*'

Penguin Modern Classics

PRICKSONGS & DESCANTS
ROBERT COOVER

With a new Introduction by Kate Atkinson

In his carnivalesque and riotously inventive *Pricksongs & Descants* Robert Coover remakes old stories: of Red Riding Hood, Hansel and Gretel, and Beauty (who married her Beast and spends a lifetime suffering his doggy stink). And he reshapes his own: a man makes repeating, re-imagined journeys in an office elevator (while his fellow riders taunt and tempt him), and in the seminal, fractal 'The Babysitter' every moment in a single night is played and replayed, every hope and threat of sex and violence done and undone. Coover's dark, wilful, comic imagination revels brilliantly in contradictions, a master of chaos.

'A marvellous magician ... a maker of miracles, a comic, a sexual tease'
The New York Times Book Review

'His is a miraculous imagination' *Newsweek*

PENGUIN MODERN CLASSICS

GERALD'S PARTY
ROBERT COOVER

With a new Introduction by Dave Eggers

Ros is dead. A bad actress but a tremendous lover, when she was alive her thighs pillowed cast members, crew, friends and acquaintances. Now Gerald's party continues around her murdered corpse (it is, after all, just the first of the night), as the guests indulge in drinking, flirting and jealousies, and the police make their brutal investigations.

Recounting an evening of cocktails, sex and violence, Robert Coover's novel is a murder mystery as rousing and disorienting as the best drunken party, a vaudevillian masterpiece.

'A hallucinogenic, phantasmagoric nightmare of mayhem and ecstasy'
The New York Times

'Filled with pratfalls, interrupted fornication, and weird rituals … perhaps even the party to end parties' Malcolm Bradbury

PENGUIN MODERN CLASSICS

COLLECTED STORIES
SAUL BELLOW

Edited by Janis Bellow with an Introduction by James Wood

'This is our greatest writer's greatest book' Martin Amis

Nobel Prize-winner Saul Bellow has deservedly been celebrated as one of the greatest modern writers. For more than sixty years he has stretched minds, imaginations, and hearts with his exhilarating perceptions of life. Here, collected for the first time in one volume and chosen by the author himself, are favourites such as 'What Kind of Day Did You Have?' and 'Leaving the Yellow House', and a previously uncollected piece, 'By the St. Lawrence'.

With his larger-than-life characters, irony, wisdom and unique humour, Bellow presents a sharp, rich, and funny world that is infinitely surprising. This is an anthology to treasure for long-time Saul Bellow fans and an excellent introduction for new readers.

WINNER OF THE NOBEL PRIZE FOR LITERATURE

PENGUIN MODERN CLASSICS

IT ALL ADDS UP
SAUL BELLOW

'Sentence by sentence, page by page, Bellow is simply the best writer we have'
The New York Times Book Review

Saul Bellow's fiction, honoured by a Nobel Prize and a Pulitzer, among other awards, has made him a literary giant. Now the man himself and a lifetime of his insightful views on a range of topics spring off the page in this, his first non-fiction collection, which encompasses articles, lectures, essays, travel pieces, and an 'Autobiography of Ideas'. *It All Adds Up* is a fascinating journey through literary America over the last forty years.

'In this rich, often provocative collection of ruminations, we witness [Bellow's] acutely perceptive mind at work, gathering, distilling and reassessing impressions of the events, people and places that shaped his life and fiction' *Miami Herald*

WINNER OF THE NOBEL PRIZE FOR LITERATURE

PENGUIN MODERN CLASSICS

THE DAY OF THE LOCUST AND **THE DREAM LIFE OF BALSO SNELL**
NATHANIEL WEST

'*The Day of the Locust* … remains the best of the Hollywood novels, a nightmare vision of humanity destroyed by its obsession with film' J. G. Ballard, *Sunday Times*

These two novellas demonstrate the fragility of the American Dream, from two very different perspectives. In *The Day of the Locust*, talented young artist Tod Hackett has been brought to Hollywood to work in the design department of a major studio. He discovers a surreal world of tarnished dreams, where violence and hysteria lurk behind the most glittering façade. Liberty and freedom have been turned into a bizarre nightmare in *The Dream Life of Balso Snell*, which focuses on the personal despair and disintegration of its protagonist, the poet Balso.

PENGUIN MODERN CLASSICS

THE BALLAD OF THE SAD CAFÉ
CARSON MCCULLERS

'Enchanting … an exquisite talent' *Sunday Times*

Few writers have expressed loneliness, the need for human understanding and the search for love with such power and poetic sensibility as the American writer Carson McCullers.

In *The Ballad of the Sad Café*, a tale of unrequited love, Miss Amelia, a spirited, unconventional woman, runs a small-town store and, except for a marriage that lasted just ten days, has always lived alone. Then Cousin Lymon appears from nowhere, a little, strutting hunchback who steals Amelia's heart. Together they transform the store into a lively, popular café. But when her rejected husband Marvin Macy returns, the result is a bizarre love triangle that brings with it violence, hatred and betrayal.

Six stories by Carson McCullers also appear in this volume.

Contemporary ... Provocative ... Outrageous ...
Prophetic ... Groundbreaking ... Funny ... Disturbing ...
Different ... Moving ... Revolutionary ... Inspiring ...
Subversive ... Life-changing ...

What makes a modern classic?

At Penguin Classics our mission has always been to make the best
books ever written available to everyone. And that also means
constantly redefining and refreshing exactly what makes a 'classic'.
That's where Modern Classics come in. Since 1961 they have been an
organic, ever-growing and ever-evolving list of books from the last
hundred (or so) years that we believe will continue to be read over and
over again.

They could be books that have inspired political dissent, such as
Animal Farm. Some, like *Lolita* or *A Clockwork Orange*, may have
caused shock and outrage. Many have led to great films, from *In Cold
Blood* to *One Flew Over the Cuckoo's Nest*. They have broken down
barriers – whether social, sexual, or, in the case of *Ulysses*, the
boundaries of language itself. And they might – like *Goldfinger* or
Scoop – just be pure classic escapism. Whatever the reason, Penguin
Modern Classics continue to inspire, entertain and enlighten millions
of readers everywhere.

'No publisher has had more influence on reading habits than Penguin'
Independent

'Penguins provided a crash course in world literature'
Guardian

The best books ever written

PENGUIN 🐧 CLASSICS

SINCE 1946

Find out more at www.penguinclassics.com